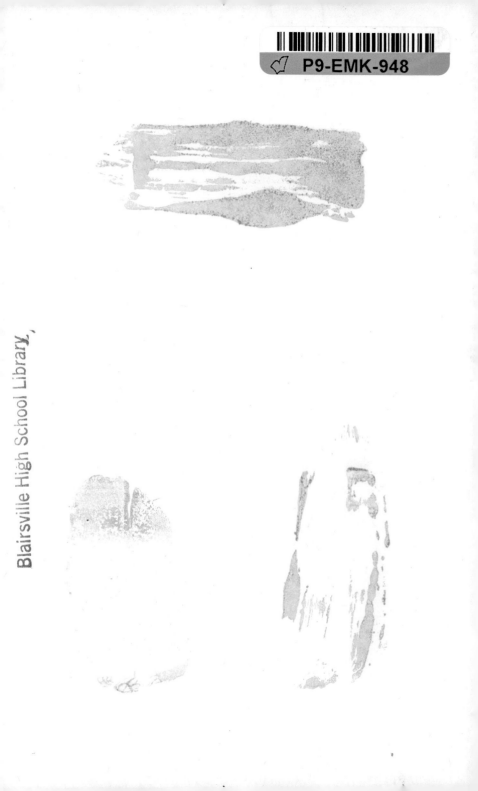

CONJURING SUMMER IN

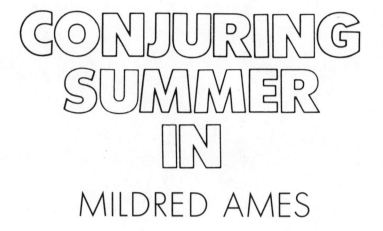

CONJURING SUMMER IN

MILDRED AMES

1 8 17

HARPER & ROW, PUBLISHERS

Cambridge, Philadelphia, San Francisco, London, Mexico City, São Paolo, Singapore, Sydney

NEW YORK

Library of Congress Cataloging-in-Publication Data
Ames, Mildred.
    Conjuring summer in.

    Summary: Sixteen-year-old Bernadette experiments
with psychic forces, including black magic, in her
unhappiness over the family's move to California; then a
series of murders and a threat on her own life ensue.
    [1. Occult sciences—Fiction. 2. Single-parent
family—Fiction] I. Title.
PZ7.A5143Co 1986   [Fic]   85-45821
ISBN 0-06-020053-7
ISBN 0-06-020054-5 (lib. bdg.)

Oh, do not tell the priest our plight,
Or he would call it a sin;
But we have been out in the woods
    all night
A-conjuring summer in.

Kipling

1

Ghosts are merely the guilt we feel toward the dead,
Keith, my stepbrother, says. I wonder if he's right.
Certainly the ghosts of that period four years ago haunt
us both. But how do you exorcise a ghost? Keith has
the answer to that, too. I must put down the whole
story on paper, right from the beginning, and exactly
as it happened. "It's therapy," he told me, "catharsis."

Keith, I feel, needs cartharsis even more than I do.
I asked him how I could put down the whole story when
there were parts I didn't know, parts only he knew. I
suggested that *he* write those.

He argued about it until I pointed out that if he
becomes a psychiatrist, he'll have to undergo a year of
therapy anyhow. I think that convinced him. "Okay,"

he said. "I'll do it, but I have to do it my way. I'll write it as though it had happened to someone else. That's the only way I can be objective."

And now that I sit here, trying to put it down from the beginning, I wonder where it *did* start. Oh, I know the time. The day of the first murder. And the place is Southern California, southwest of Los Angeles in a town called Cerritos Beach, where Mother, Keith, and I had lived for several months.

But for me it started earlier, way back in Willow Orchard, when Gran would gather herbs from her garden and brew up teas (*tisanes*, she called them) that could send a bellyache right back to wherever it came from. Not only that; Gran always seemed to have the answer to everything. When people asked her how she managed to look a good fifteen years younger than her age, she said, "I drink a *tisane* of chamomile and angelica every morning of my life." What she didn't tell them was that she also had her own secret potion, which she used on her face before going to bed every night. "No need to give away all my magic secrets," she told me.

I said, "Oh, Gran, you don't really believe in magic, do you?"

"Of course I believe in magic," she said, sounding so sincere, I knew she meant it.

I wondered if she was right. Then just before my tenth birthday I confided to her that I desperately wanted

4

a very expensive English riding habit. "Mother says it's out of the question," I told her. "She says she doesn't want to hear another word about it."

"Just how badly do you want this outfit?"

"Oh, Gran, I'd die for it." I had visions of Wilson Curtis, the boy I liked, seeing me in it and thinking that I looked like a heroine right out of *National Velvet.*

"You want it that badly, eh? Well, I'd say that calls for a bit of magic."

"I don't understand."

"Look here, now." She reached into the deep pocket of the old sweater she had on and pulled out a change purse.

"I didn't mean I wanted you to give me the money, Gran," I said quickly.

"Lord love you, I don't have that kind of money to give anyone. No, but I've got something just as good." She took a piece of folded tissue paper from the purse and opened it. "This just happens to be a very special four-leaf clover, picked by the light of a full moon. Do you know what that means?"

I shook my head.

"A four-leaf clover picked by the light of a full moon grants one wish to the wisher. Since this one has never been wished upon, I give it to you."

I took it, but I didn't really believe until the day of my birthday, when I opened my presents and found the exact outfit I had wanted. Ralph, my stepfather, had bought it for me, and Gran swore she wasn't the one who'd told him what I'd wanted. Forever after I believed in magic.

On the day of the murder, I was fourteen and delving into a more sophisticated magic than herb brewing, the kind of magic that could help me take control of my life, could make things come out the way I wanted them to come out. That fall day comes back to me now with a clarity that's almost startling. I can even remember what was running through my mind as I came home from school.

All afternoon everyone had talked about the murder of a girl hardly older than I. Murders are commonplace enough in these times, but they seem like fiction until one happens close to home. This one had taken place on the Peninsula, an area of hills that rose only a short distance from the bungalow we rented on the ocean side of Pacific Coast Highway. The hideous crime seemed all the more reason for hating Southern California, for desperately wanting to return to Willow Orchard.

I remember the bleak feeling that filled me as I walked along. I tried to blot it out by concentrating on the jewel names of the streets in my neighborhood. Jewels were amulets that protected against all kinds of hazards, I told myself, jade against lightning, ruby against witchcraft, topaz against the Evil Eye. I was comforted until I came to Onyx Street. Then I hurried across. Onyx always meant bad luck.

What a relief to reach my own front door! Before going inside, I checked the mailbox. When I saw *Miss Bernadette McKay* in a hand that looked as if someone had written it with spider fingers, I felt my heartbeat quicken. Gran.

I held the letter to my cheek for a moment, imagining I could smell the rosemary from her garden. "Rosemary's for remembrance," she always said. "Did you know that, lovey? Nothing better for the complexion. Takes away evil dreams, too." Then she'd look around her unruly garden and vaguely add, "Oh, yes, and very good against moths."

From her childhood pictures I could see that I looked a lot like Gran when she was my age. We had the same dark hair and eyes, the same deep cleft in our chins, and what my mother said was the same stubborn set to our jaws. I didn't mind looking like Gran, but I regretted the fact that I was also her height, five foot one. I longed to be tall and willowy.

How I had hated leaving Gran and the friends I'd known all my life! During my first weeks in California, I had cried myself to sleep every night. Although I was tempted now to rip open Gran's letter and read it right away, I tucked it in a schoolbook to save for the privacy of my own room.

I took out the rest of the mail from the box and noticed a pink envelope also addressed to me. If I hadn't recognized the handwriting as Debbie Maxwell's, my best friend in Willow Orchard, I would have known by the smell that it had come from her. She always perfumed her letters with her mother's expensive perfume. Debbie read romances. She used to say it was very important for a woman to have a scent that everyone identified with her. I put her letter with Gran's.

Inside the house, I missed the usual banging of Keith's typewriter. This was his first year in community college. He always tried to complete his homework in the afternoon in case a call came for him from The Broadway Department Store, where he clerked part-time.

I left Mother's mail on the kitchen table, then went on down the hall to stop outside the open door of Keith's room. His portable sat on the desk, books and papers scattered all around it, but Keith's long, thin body lay stretched out on the bed, Grit, our marmalade tomcat, curled up on his chest. Keith stared glumly at the ceiling, hands locked behind his dark head. I noticed a book on abnormal psychology discarded beside him. Which was nothing unusual. He was always reading such books to see if he was sufficiently intrigued to major in what he jokingly called the disturbed sciences.

"Where's Mother?" I asked.

He turned his head in my direction. "She's gone to the store. The boss man's taking dinner with us."

"Mother's boss? Don?"

"Who else?"

I felt first annoyed, then suspicious. "He owns four

8

restaurants. Why can't he eat at one of those?"

"I imagine because Louise asked him to eat here. Maybe he's sick of Mexican food."

Mother was hostess at El Bandido, Don's restaurant in the town center of Cerritos Beach, an area everyone called The Village. "You'd think he'd feed *her*. He can afford it better than we can." When Keith refused to comment, I couldn't help voicing my fears. "I'll bet it's not the food he's interested in. I'll bet it's Mother."

Keith eyed me curiously for a moment; then his heavy, black brows settled in a frown. "I think you're having delusions." I hoped with all my heart he was right. I changed the subject. "Did you hear about the murder?"

"The hitchhiker? I read something about it."

I went into his room and perched on the edge of his desk chair. "Her throat was cut, Keith. And practically in our own neighborhood." When I felt myself shiver, I did what I always did to shut out the whole miserable California scene. I concentrated on Willow Orchard, our town in Ohio, with its huge oak trees that met to form shady arches over the streets. In my imagination I saw again the house where we'd lived when my step-father was alive, Gran's garden with her many cats rolling, drunk, in the catnip; and for a moment everything ugly went away. But only for a moment. "I hate living here," I said. "I wish we'd never come. I wish we were back in Willow Orchard."

A glimmer of interest stirred in Keith's eyes now.

9

"Why? Just because a girl got murdered?"

"That's one of the reasons. Awful things happen around here every day. And you never feel as if you belong—I mean, it's not like home. At home everybody knows you and cares about you. Here nobody cares."

"You know, it's only natural to feel insecure in a new place. But you'll get over it."

"I don't know whether I feel insecure or not, but I sure don't feel like anybody out here. At home I always got big parts in all the shows we put on in school. Teachers always said I had a nice voice. I just tried out for a Gilbert and Sullivan operetta here, and I didn't even make the chorus!"

"That's too bad. But that doesn't mean you don't have a nice voice—you do. They just haven't found out yet. And remember, everybody knew our family back there. Dad was an important contractor. I'm not saying you did, but maybe—just maybe—once in a while you got a little preferential treatment."

I snorted. I knew there was some truth in what he said, but I wasn't about to admit it.

"Wait until you're a few years older. You'll be glad you're out of that hick town—everybody watching every move you make. Besides, murder can happen anyplace, even in Willow Orchard."

"Well, it never did."

"Maybe not in our time. . . . Anyhow, psychiatrists

believe that when people get murdered, it's because they generally ask for it. They seem to have some deep-seated emotional need to make victims of themselves. If this girl hadn't been hitchhiking, which she had to know was like playing Russian roulette, nothing would have happened to her."

Keith always had psychological theories about everybody. I put it down to all those books he read. I couldn't argue with him, though, because I didn't know as much as he did about that kind of thing.

His eyes narrowed the way his father's used to when he was reprimanding me. "I don't want you hitching rides—ever!"

"Oh, Keith! That's what I mean—you're changing. You never used to be so bossy. You'd think you were my father." I let out a deep sigh. "It's California. We're all changing. At home no one had to worry about getting murdered when they got a ride with somebody."

"Well, here you do, so don't try it."

I glanced at him, annoyed and at the same time touched. I knew that, too often, he felt Mother and I were his responsibility these days. That was more of a burden than either of us expected him to bear. I said, "How come you're in bed?"

"I'm not *in* bed. I'm on the bed." He rubbed Grit's head absently. "I'm tired. I worked last night—late."

"That's what I mean about changing. You never used to flop down in the afternoon." I sighed again. "This

11

place will change all of us." I got up and dragged off to my room.

After she'd left, Keith thought about what Bernadette had said. Was she exaggerating her fears about Louise and Don's relationship because she was so desperate to return to Willow Orchard? She'd never really wanted to come out here in the first place, the way he and Louise had. Louise had told her, "We'll try it. If we just can't stand it, we'll move back home."

The trouble with Bernadette was she was suffering from feelings of insecurity. Which was only natural. With his father's death they had all lost the security he'd provided. Then, too, she'd just about been Queen of the May back home. Everyone had given her all kinds of attention that she wasn't getting out here. That included him. He felt guilty about that, but there just wasn't the time anymore. Back there he hadn't been working and going to school, too.

He *had* been on the debating team, though. He smiled now, remembering how mad Bernadette used to get when he had to stay after school and couldn't join her in taking out old man Walgren's horses for exercise. She seemed to think those excursions were a big deal.

Well, come to think of it, so did he. They'd ride the horses out to Sutter's Pond and she'd talk about all her weighty problems, like why Wilson Curtis never asked her to dance at Cotillion, and he'd have to explain all about the psyches of little boys. Sometimes they'd have their let's-talk-about-*life* days, which could cover everything from antisocial behavior to the nature of love. He had made up half the stuff he told her, but she'd never seemed to suspect. The five-year difference in their ages made him the authority. Yet at that point how much did he really know about *life*? He had to admit, though, made up or not, all the answers he spouted out to her very sincere questions made him feel mature and, yes, important. The guru syndrome? Probably.

He could understand how she felt about going back to a life that had once been good. What she couldn't understand was that it could never be the same again. Not without his father. He felt the tears come to his eyes.

He hoped now that there was nothing to her suspicions about Louise and Don. As far as Keith was concerned, Louise would always belong to his father.

I settled myself on the bed to read Gran's letter, hoping it would dispel some of my gloom. She was my father's mother, my real father, who died in the Vietnam War before I ever had the chance to know him. Although she had come to this country when she was eleven years old, somehow she had never lost her English accent. She had bright, lively eyes and a mind that could wonder at the vein of a leaf; delicate little hands that could plow up a garden, soothe a feverish forehead, or crack a flea between their nails. Constantly, she bustled around as if there were so many exciting things to see, to do, to discover, that she was afraid she might miss one of them if she rested. I kept all her letters, as she kept mine. This is the one that came that day:

Dearest Bernadette,

You can't miss me any more than I miss you, lovey. Well, you would all go off to California, where I'll never even get a peek at you again because I'm too old to go traveling by bus or train and not even God Himself will get me on an airplane.

Well, I'm just being selfish. I know if Ralph hadn't died, you'd all still be here. He was a good stepfather to you, Ralph was, though I never did approve of the adoption. He's Keith's father, not yours. You're a Crenshaw, not a McKay. You just remember that. Still, I mourn Ralph's passing because you're of an age where a girl needs a father. What a pity that you never had the chance to know your own.

Well, we'd all like to make the world over, but I suppose there's no changing what is. I feel sorry for your poor mother. Losing two husbands to tragedy is more than any woman deserves. I only pray that someday she will find the happiness that's due her. I hope you help her all you can. And Keith, too. Give my regards to both of them.

> *With lots of love and hugs,*
> *I am as always,*
> *Your loving Gran*

What Gran didn't know was that the adoption was my idea. I just didn't want to have a different name from theirs. That seemed very important at the time. After all, if they were all McKays and I wasn't, then I felt I wasn't really part of the family.

Although I had loved Ralph and had always thought of him as my father, now that he was dead, I began fantasizing about my own father. My dreams went something like this:

One dreary evening the doorbell rings. I answer it. A man in a trench coat stands there, his eyes soft and misty. "My Bernadette. . . ." he whispers. "And lovelier than I'd ever dreamed. Don't you know me, daughter?"

"Father!" I exclaim. (Never "Dad.") I throw myself into his arms and we embrace, both weeping silently. Then Mother appears behind me. "James," she murmurs, choking a little on the name. Their eyes meet and lock for one unfathomable moment. My father releases me and bounds to her side. She extends a hand. His own closes around it lovingly.

"They kept me prisoner all these years, Louise," he says. "But now I am free. I have come to take you and Bernadette home with me, home to Willow Orchard, where we'll live out our days in *peace* and *love*."

"And where we'll all be *safe*," I add.

"But Keith—" Mother says.

My father says, "Ah, yes, Keith. I understand he's

15

McKay's boy by another marriage. My mother told me the whole story. I want you to know that I don't hold anything against you. I'm only glad you had someone to take care of you for all the years I've been gone. Ralph McKay, I hear, treated my daughter as if she were his own child. I intend to do the same with his son."

Naturally my dream always ended with all of us flying off into the sunrise on the next plane out of Los Angeles.

When we had first come out here, I hadn't realized how my life would change. At home I was Ralph McKay's daughter. Everyone respected him, not only because he was a good person but because he was the most important contractor in town. He knew the mayor and everyone else who was anybody. When people called me the McKay girl, I felt important, too. Out here I was just another kid in a school with, as far as I was concerned, too many kids there already.

Not only that, but my relationship with Keith and Mother had changed since we'd been in California. With her working and Keith always tied up with his job or his schoolwork, neither one of them ever seemed to have time for me anymore. We all had been so much closer back there.

I opened Debbie's letter. As I started to read, I was overwhelmed by a feeling of homesickness. She talked about all the people we knew and brought me up-to-

16

date on all the gossip. When I came to nearly the end of her letter, I almost gasped in disbelief. "You remember Wilson Curtis," it read. "He's got the part of King Arthur in the play we're doing this year. I tried out, and can you believe it, I got the part of Guinevere!! Wilson says we'll just have to rehearse together. He's been walking me home every day after school and coming into the house, where we read our lines. He's cute. And you know what else? I think he likes me!! Know what I mean?"

With that, I stopped reading. Did I remember Wilson Curtis? He was only the person I was going to marry when I grew up, that's all. Debbie knew exactly how I felt about him. He had curly black hair and the bluest eyes of anyone I knew except Keith. Like me, he always got one of the good roles in anything we put on in school. I felt we had so much in common, and I always thought he did too. And even now, I still believed he'd liked me, though I'd written him two letters since I'd been out here and he hadn't answered either. Some people just didn't write letters, I'd told myself.

I tore up Debbie's letter and threw it into my wastebasket. I swore never to write her again. How could I ever have once thought of her as my best friend? After that I had a good cry.

At dinner that night Keith could tell that Don was interested in Louise. Which was probably to be ex-

17

pected. Don was divorced and Louise was a widow. And not just any widow. Louise had a quality about her that made her seem vulnerable. People always seemed to want to take care of her, especially men. The paternal syndrome. They'd rush to open doors for her, or to give her their seats, or to carry her bundles. And when it happened, she had a special gift for acting as if every time was a first time. Then too, she was very pretty in a kind of breathless, always-at-sixes-and-sevens way.

That night Don showed all the telltale signs, Keith thought. His eyes rested on her too often and too long; his voice, which usually sounded like a hearty boom, had a special gentleness in it; and he hung on her every word as if phrases like "Please pass the salt" were gems of wisdom. Anyhow, there were enough signs to worry Keith. And Don was a big solid man, more like a boulder than a rock. From the way Louise asked his advice, Keith was afraid she was already beginning to lean on that solidness.

At one point Louise said to Keith, "Do you know anything about the tarot class Bernadette wants to start tonight?"

"Tarot class!" he exclaimed. He was well aware that since they'd lived in California, Bernadette had become more and more interested in the occult, reading books about witchcraft and carrying good-luck charms with her wherever she went. The thing he liked least about the state was that it seemed to attract every bizarre cult in the country. "Bernadette is superstitious enough without fooling with tarot cards."

"I am not superstitious," Bernadette retorted.

"Oh, yes, you are. If you don't watch out, you'll turn into an obsessive-compulsive," he said.

Bernadette said, "I wish you'd stop spouting all that Freud stuff. I don't even know what you're talking about, and I don't think you do either."

"I'm talking about a mental illness. An obsessive-compulsive is a rigid person who is not up to meeting the challenges of life and tries to organize the world in any way he or she can to avoid anxiety."

"Who's trying to avoid anxiety? I've got plenty of anxiety."

"Then face your anxieties in a healthy way instead of using a bunch of silly cards to tell you whether or not you should go out of the house."

They argued until Louise said, "I wish you two wouldn't bicker in front of guests."

Don said, "I'm not a guest. I'm a friend of the family," and turned a kindly smile on Bernadette. "That class sounds like it might be a lot of fun. Tarot cards are fortune-telling cards, aren't they?"

"Yes," Bernadette said, looking surprised that he even knew.

"I had an old aunt who used to tell fortunes. Shook me up·sometimes how close she'd hit the mark," he said.

"Well, I suppose there's no harm in it if it's only done for fun," Louise said to him. "Still, I don't want Bernadette out on the streets by herself at night. Why, only last night a girl was murdered just a few miles from here. It's not safe."

Don said, "I know. I read about it in the papers. Well, kids *will* hitch rides."

"Mother, if I can't be out at night, how am I going to get there?" Bernadette asked impatiently.

"You know I can't take you. Both Don and I have to be at work by seven. You said the class didn't start until eight."

"Just where is this place?" Don asked.

Louise said, "In a little shop in The Village called, of all things, The Mandrake Root. Eva, the woman who runs the shop, I've met at PTA. Her daughter, Francine, is in Bernadette's class. Eva seems very nice. She sells occult supplies—whatever those are. Books and candles mostly, I guess."

"How am I going to get there?" Bernadette persisted.

Don had the answer. "I'll bet Keith would be glad to drive his little sister—pick her up later, too. That's what big brothers are for, isn't it, Keith?"

Keith felt a stab of resentment. What was the guy trying to do? Run their family? "I don't know if I'll be able to—my car's been acting up."

Louise turned to Bernadette. "If Keith can't take you, you won't be able to go. I just won't have you out at night by yourself."

Bernadette said to him, "Please, Keith. I really want to take this class. I've been planning on it for weeks now."

He didn't mind giving her the ride. What he did mind was that Don had suggested it. Keith was kicking himself because he hadn't spoken up sooner. Now it would seem as if he were obeying Don. Yet if he refused, he would just be taking his resentment out on his sister. Finally, he said, "Oh, all right, if it means that much to you. Just remember, I don't approve. And pray my car holds together."

When Don beamed at all of them, Keith felt he was sending strong fatherly vibrations around the table. Worse than that, Louise's smile seemed to drink them in. Keith didn't like the look of the situation at all.

After Don and Mother left for work, I hurried to my room and my dresser. Beneath my underwear, I dug out the drawing I had finished and tried out yesterday.

On a huge sheet of paper, I had drawn a large circle with a smaller circle a little inside it to frame a five-pointed star, or pentagram. One of the pentagram's points shot toward the top of the circle, two toward the bottom, because the books I had read said that that was the position to repel evil. A reversed pentagram—with two points upward—was a symbol of the devil.

I had put in the proper astrological signs to accomplish my purpose. The sign of the favorable planet, and the sign of the spirit belonging to that planet, I had drawn between the two circles. The name of the planet's spirit was at the bottom, as it should be, and the name of its demon or intelligence at the top. The Hebrew characters I had so carefully copied expressed the thought *My will be done.* I had done as the books said and made my drawing when the chosen planet was exhibiting a favorable aspect.

Last night, in the eerie light of flickering candles, I had unfolded the paper, placed it on the floor, and stood within the circle. The heavy scent of incense burning in a saucer on my dresser filled my nostrils and gave me a heady feeling. Trembling, I read from a book of incantations I'd bought at The Mandrake Root. Chanting, I said, "I conjure and command thee, O spirit Astaroth. Come at once from whatever part of the world, come, fulfill my desires and persist unto the end in accordance with my will. I conjure thee by Him to Whom all creatures are obedient, by the Ineffable Name Tetragrammaton Jehovah, by which Name all the hosts of things in heaven, of things in earth, of things in hell, do tremble and are confounded."

I had stood quiet within my circle, feeling a cold chill creep up my spine. I had imagined that instead of incense, I was smelling the hot fires of hell. Had I known then what was to come, I would have said the sensation was far more than mere imagination.

When nothing happened, I repeated the incantation over and over, waiting for a sign, but there was none.

Then, when I was just about to give up, the lights in our house went out for just a few seconds, then flashed back on. That was my sign! I had called up one of the Lords of Darkness, Astaroth, fourth in the chain of command. I had been too frightened to go any higher.

In my strongest and most fearless-sounding voice, I commanded him to arrange a way for Mother, Keith, and me to go back to Willow Orchard, a way that would be satisfactory to everyone involved.

When I was sure I had made myself absolutely clear, I read aloud the formula to send him back. "O spirit Astaroth, because thou hast answered my demands, I hereby license thee to depart. Go, I say, but be ready and willing to come whenever duly conjured by the rites of magic. I conjure thee to withdraw in peace, and may the peace of God ever continue between me and thee. Amen."

I had heard a sudden gust of wind outdoors and taken it for a sign that the demon had departed. With a big sigh of relief, I'd stepped outside the circle, refolded the paper with my pentagram, and hidden it away.

Now as I returned it to the drawer once more, the thought occurred to me that if Mother or Keith discovered my drawing, neither of them would know what it meant. But I knew. And the thought brought a chill. The old wizards, the necromancers I had read about, had, like me, used their pentagrams to call up the demons out of hell to make their pacts. The magician

23

stood within his circle for protection. One step outside before the spell was broken, the demons sent back, and he was doomed. But my pentagram was different, I told myself, because it was in a good cause.

2

Signs of the zodiac, many of them framed like paintings, decorated The Mandrake Root. Books on occultism lined the walls. Amulets, zodiac medals, and tiny crystal balls on dainty gold chains dangled from a jewelry rack. More disturbing, perhaps, was the glass urn of mandrake root. The Arabs called it the devil's testicles, I'd read. But everything about the shop fascinated me. Even the apothecary jars of powdered incense that had names like Dragon's Blood and John the Conqueror.

The small store was already full of people when, a little late, I slid onto one of the folding chairs near the exit. Keith's car had given trouble all the way. I had left him outside, fooling with the engine. As I waited for things to start, I toyed with the plain pine box that held my tarot cards.

Giselle Fox, the young woman who worked in the shop, had assured me when I'd bought it that the box would keep my cards free of other people's vibrations. She came out of a back room now, ready to begin the class. Dark eyes and hair, olive skin, and golden hoops swinging from her ears gave her the look of a gypsy. A band held back her long, straight hair and matched a suede vest caught together only at the breasts, opening below to show bare skin. On her cheek, small enough to look like a beauty mark, she had drawn a sun sign, the bowman Sagittarius. She looked sensational.

"Tonight," Giselle said, "we're going to take only the first five cards of the Major Arcana and the four cards of the Minor Arcana that go with each. Isn't that a super word—Arcana? It means secrets or mysteries." She smiled, and deep, elfish dimples appeared in her cheeks. "And isn't that why you're all here? To unravel the secrets of the future? To learn about the mysteries?"

Giselle went on to tell us how to shuffle the cards and how to pick them up the right way. She said, "Sometimes I make a mistake and pick up the cards wrong. But if my soul told me to do it that way, then it's right." Her dark eyes grew very serious and her voice grew solemn. "Your soul *knows*. Souls aren't wrong—people are. I made a deal with my soul, and whichever way it comes out, that's the way it's supposed to be. So make a deal with *your* soul and it will be all right for you, too."

She then held up the first card, The Magician. "This is the Will card—the human will. It stands for the things you want."

I found the card in my pack, a yellow card with a red-robed man holding a wand high over his head.

The second card, The High Priestess, Giselle told us, was Enlightenment of the Will—learning about or learning how to get what you wanted.

The third, The Empress, stood for action—doing what you'd learned in order to get what you wanted.

"Now it's up to you what you want," she said. "Want the right things and you can get them. But if what you want is something bad—bad is just a great big circle. It comes right back to you."

A man's voice said, "There's a sayin', Giselle—the evils you do one by one come back to you two by two."

"That's absolutely right, Sammy," she said.

I recognized Sammy Rupp, a psychic I knew from the shop. I was surprised to see him there, because I knew he already read cards.

The fourth card, The Emperor, stood for the realization of the first three cards, or finally getting what you wanted.

The fifth, The Hierophant, symbolized the law of universal order, or the idea that what you give out comes back to you in kind, sometimes twofold.

Giselle said, "Now, remember, when you read cards, it doesn't mean that things *have* to turn out the way the cards say. It means that up to now, the way things are going, if they keep on going the same way, that's the way they're bound to turn out unless you change them. And you *can* change them. It's all up to you."

She tapped her head with her forefinger. "All in here. If things are going wrong, it's because of the way you're thinking. Straighten out your head and you'll straighten out your life. *You* make your life what it is. It's up to you whether you make it a fantastic thing or you bum it. Remember the lines about the two men who looked out of prison bars?"

Someone said, "One saw mud and one saw stars."

Giselle nodded soberly. "And that's the way it is. It's what you *think*. Things are the way you see them."

Soon after, we broke for a rest period. While people started to push out toward the street, I gathered up my things. As I got up from my aisle seat, a tall, thin boy charged forward, stopping short to miss me. Then someone bumped him from behind, pushing him headlong into my arms. Looking as if the contact had contaminated him, he instantly recoiled. A moment later I noticed a small notebook on the floor and immediately rescued it from the tread of oncoming feet. A crush of people kept me from chasing after him, so I dropped the book into my tote bag, intending to return it to him after the break.

The shop had almost emptied when my friend Francine joined me. Although her mother owned the The

Mandrake Root, Francine had never learned to read cards. Until I'd talked her into taking the class with me, she'd always said the cards took too much time to learn.

I think I liked Francine because she was so different from me. Where I shied away from excitement, she seemed to thrive on it. And she was fun, because she thought up so many wild things to do, things I would never have dared do by myself. Once we even went mud sliding. Whenever she suggested doing something that I thought was outrageous, I'd say, "Oh, no, I couldn't possibly do anything like that." Somehow she'd always talk me into it, and afterward I was glad. Everything I did with her seemed like a big adventure.

And I loved her mother's shop. I'd always been drawn to magic, probably because of Gran, but I hated to admit it because most people think you're crazy. Especially people like Keith. And one of the things that was very important to me was his approval.

When I first met Francine, she introduced me to the shop and took me around, pointing out all the interesting objects that could satisfy your deepest wishes. There were even wax candles made in the shapes of human figures. "If you want someone to fall in love with you," she said, "you burn the red one and concentrate on the person. If you just want something good to happen to someone, you burn the white one. There are even black ones to make bad things happen to people, but of course we don't sell those. We don't believe in black magic."

I said, "You don't really believe that something like burning a candle can make anything happen, do you?"

"Of course. Look, right now, think of something you want, and I'll tell you how to get it."

I laughed.

"I mean it," she said.

I decided I might as well play along with her. "Well, okay—how can I get better grades in algebra?"

She picked up one of the candles we'd been looking at, a white one. "This is Mr. Hanley, our beloved teacher. Burn this every time you get a chance and concentrate on what you just said, only tell it to him in your mind. Try it and see what happens."

"Nothing, I'll bet."

"Just try it," she insisted. "What do you have to lose?"

"Nothing, I guess. Okay, I'll try it."

So I bought one of the candles shaped like a human figure, and every day I burned it for about five minutes and, feeling very foolish, said to the thing, "Please, Mr. Hanley, I need help. I just don't seem to be getting anyplace in algebra."

About a week later, when the head, shoulders, and most of the torso of my candle had disappeared, Mr. Hanley asked me to stay after class. "I think you need help with your algebra," he said. "If you can stay a couple of afternoons next week, I imagine I can straighten you out."

Oh, wow! I said to myself. The thing really worked. He even used some of the words I'd said in my mind. I was shaken by the power that rested in something as innocent as a candle, as well as in the mind.

Francine drew me away from the past now as she said, "Let's go over to the pizza place and get a Coke." Her hands parted a long, blond, silky mane and pulled both sides back from her eyes as if she were opening draperies.

"Wait a minute. Here's Sammy," I said.

Sammy, a big, chubby man, in his late thirties, lumbered up beside us, his gait hulking and heavy, like a bear's. His round face broke into the smile of a baby-book cherub. "Oh, hi, Bernadette." A great callused longshoreman's hand reached up to smooth back his already slick, dark hair. Fuzzy, reddish sideburns looked as if they had been purchased as an afterthought and glued onto his cheeks.

Francine shifted impatiently as I said, "What are you doing here, Sammy? You already know how to read cards."

He shrugged his powerful shoulders. "I can always learn somethin' new, y'know. Giselle and me, we learn from each other. She comes down to my apartment or I go up to hers. We study on things together."

"Giselle is wonderful," I said. "Like yours, Sammy, her soul is pure."

Sammy's ponderous nod agreed.

"How's Michael?" I asked as Francine took my arm and tried to hurry me on.

"Michael says you got a lotta ESP, Bernadette. You could maybe even get to be a healer if you worked at it."

Francine said, "See you later, Sammy," and pulled me toward the door. Sammy smiled his cherub's smile again and waved us off.

Outside, a full autumn moon lit the night sky and cast an eerie light over the street. Francine said, "Who's Michael?"

"I can't believe you don't know."

"Well, I don't."

"Everybody in the shop knows about Michael. You just haven't been spending enough time there."

"I know, but I just can't stand my stepfather, and he always seems to be around the shop these days."

Her stepfather was a former wrestler who often worked behind the counter and also held classes in the psychic sciences. "I didn't know you didn't like Steve."

"I hate him. He's so gross."

I sometimes wondered if one of the reasons Francine and I had become friends was because we both had complicated families. Someplace along the way we had lost some of the original members and picked up others. But then, it seemed to me that all the families out here were complicated. Everybody seemed to have at least two sets of parents and as many sets of brothers or sisters. Perhaps that was what made Mother feel we belonged here.

Francine persisted. "Who's Michael?"

"You know Sammy does automatic writing. He goes into a trance and lets the spirit write through him. He says Michael's one of the archangels who communicates with him."

"You mean there's more than one?"

"Well, sure. Sammy says he has three spirits. Two are archangels and one is somebody named Jacob. They tell him all kinds of things, sometimes in Latin."

"Sammy can't even speak English."

"Giselle translates for him. She went to Berkeley, you know. She's pretty smart."

Francine snorted. "She may be smart that way, but she wasn't smart enough to get child support for her kids when she got divorced." She shook her head disapprovingly. "Come on. Let's get our Cokes." We started up the street, but after a few steps she stopped abruptly. "Now wait a minute. You told me Giselle said we shouldn't fool with Ouija boards or do automatic writing—that we'd only call up bad spirits that way."

"I know I did. She said you get dirty little disembodied spirits that float around close to earth on the astral plane—murderers and atheists." As I said the words I thought I felt a clammy hand brush my cheek. In another moment I realized it was only a moist breeze

33

from the ocean, which was only a few blocks away. I relaxed and added, "But she said it was all right for Sammy to use the Ouija board, because his soul is so pure—he only attracts the higher types of spirits."

I had never thought much about spirits or that kind of thing before I met Giselle, but she knew so much about the subject and was so convincing, I just had to believe her.

"Oh," Francine said, sounding as if she had lost interest in spirits and Ouija boards. "Let's hurry up."

To my surprise, Keith was still outside, working on the small rear engine of his VW. And getting no place, it seemed. The car still sputtered and coughed. Francine spotted him and, like a one-woman army, advanced. I could see Keith try to bury his head deep in an engine that was anything but deep.

"Hi, Keith," she trilled. "Having trouble?"

Francine had something of a crush on Keith, but for some reason I couldn't figure out, he just didn't like her. In a cool voice, he said, "Whatever gave you that idea?"

She looked surprised and hurt.

I said, "I could have told you Keith has a short fuse when he's doing anything on that car."

"Someone having trouble?" Giselle, carrying a paper cup, appeared from behind us.

I saw Keith stare at her. Gape was probably a better word. In her skimpy suede vest she had quite a lot to gape at, and there was enough light from the stores to guarantee that no one missed any of it. "Engine's giving me a little trouble," he said, as if it wasn't obvious.

"Keith is Bernadette's brother," Francine said.

I introduced them, and Giselle said, "All of us in the shop just love Bernadette."

"You work there?" Keith asked her.

Francine giggled. "She's the hired help."

"That's right," Giselle said. "Tonight I'm the teacher, but I clerk there days."

"Every day?" he asked.

"Every day except Monday."

Keith nodded in a way that made me think he was carefully cataloguing the information for future reference. Then he glanced at Francine and me, wiped his dirty hands on an equally dirty rag, dug down in his pocket, and pulled out some change. "Here." He thrust some coins at me. "You and Francine have a Coke on me."

I suspected he was trying to get rid of us, so I said to Giselle, "Why don't you come with us?"

She held up her paper cup. "I have mine. And you'd better hurry. We'll be going back in a few minutes."

"Come on," Francine said. "If we don't step on it, we won't get anything."

I refused to budge. Francine coming on to Keith was one thing, but Keith coming on to Giselle, or vice versa, was something else. In spite of the fact that I thought her wonderful, she was years older than Keith. Besides, I didn't want him to get involved with someone out here any more than I wanted Mother to get involved with Don. They'd never want to go back home then.

When I didn't leave, Keith glanced from me to Francine, seeming at a loss.

Finally Giselle broke the silence. "I like the color of your car."

"It's candy-apple red—custom paint job. You should see it in the daylight." Now that he had latched onto a subject, he began to warm to it. "In fact, the whole car's custom—upholstery, steering wheel, accessories. Even the engine's been hopped up with custom parts."

"Super," Giselle said. "Did *you* do it?"

He looked a little crushed. "Well, no—I bought it used."

She started walking around the car, taking it all in. "What a great buy."

He immediately brightened. He'd now forgotten Francine and me. He trailed after Giselle like a used-car salesman, opening and slamming doors, pointing up unique features, jumping up and down on the special bumper. I knew how Keith felt about that car, but this was really disgusting.

"What kind of trouble are you having with the engine?" she asked.

Now he drew himself up until he quite towered above her. With all the superiority of the mechanically initiated, he said, "I don't know how much you know about customizing—"

"Not a thing."

36

Ah!

He said, "Well, you see, when a car has as many custom parts as this one—and I mean sensitive, complex parts made to fine tolerances—well, it's bound to be a little temperamental."

"Oh?"

"Oh, yes. See here . . ." He took her over to the engine and the three of us had to endure a short and boring education on the machining of special parts.

"I wish I had time to hear more," Giselle said.

"Anytime," Keith offered.

Giselle turned to Francine and me. "Come on, you two. It's time to go back." She put an arm around each of us and headed us toward the shop. I glanced around once to see a silly grin on Keith's face as he stared after us. *Disgusting.*

By the time the class broke up, the VW's engine sounded better. After we took off, Keith swung around by the ocean to test his work on the open boulevard.

I sighed impatiently but sank back into my seat as he zoomed up the road. A fine mist veiled the ocean now and descended over everything with a damp chill. I drew my sweater closer around me as Keith cracked his window to let in the sound of pounding surf. He drank in hearty breaths of salt air.

I shivered. "Could you close the window?"

"Salt air is good for you," Keith said, but he rolled

up the window. "That girl I was talking to tonight—what did you say her name was?"

"Giselle?"

"That's the one. Kind of an unusual name."

"She changed it."

"Oh? Why?"

"She gets better vibrations this way."

He snorted. "Vibrations!"

"Yes. She changed her name because of numerology. In numerology, Giselle Fox vibrates to the number six, which, she feels, is an awfully good number, because you can divide it by two and by three. That way she gets all the qualities of six and some of the qualities of two and three."

"Good God! How did you find out all that stuff?"

"She told me."

"And you'll believe anything. She was putting you on. Don't you have any sense of humor? All I had to do was talk to her for five minutes and I could tell she wasn't like the other neurotic nuts that believe in that kind of mumbo jumbo."

I lapsed into stony silence. Finally I said, "Giselle's really very nice—for her age."

"How old is she?"

"Almost thirty."

"Aw, come on—she's not that old."

"Well, she must be. After all, she's divorced and she has two kids. That takes time."

Now Keith fell silent.

I said, "She seems so nice, too. I mean, you'd think she could hold a husband. But I suppose you never know all about a person just by talking to them. I mean, a person can be nice to know and just awful to live with."

"Plenty of people are divorced these days."

"Oh, I know. And it could be the husband's fault. But of course you always wonder . . . I mean, I like Giselle, but sometimes—well, like tonight—that outfit she had on might be all right someplace, but if you're going to teach something, how can you expect people to pay attention if you're practically naked?"

"You're suggesting that she's an exhibitionist, that she has a compulsive need to—"

"I am?" I said.

"You are, and you're wrong. That's not exhibition-ism, it's showmanship. It's a good way to pack a class."

"Just the same, though, it doesn't seem right to dress like a stripteaser when you're teaching a serious sub-ject."

Keith fell silent again, thoughtfully silent.

As he turned off the ocean boulevard, I suddenly remembered the notebook I'd picked up. I'd meant to return it to its owner but had somehow completely for-gotten. I hoped there was nothing important in it, be-cause now I wouldn't be able to give it back until the following week.

3

On Saturday morning while Keith, Mother, and I had breakfast, I kept thinking of my pentagram. I was certain that if I had done everything right, and I was sure I had, it would work eventually. Then why did I feel so depressed and guilty? I wasn't asking for anything that could possibly hurt anyone.

"Is Francine coming by this afternoon?" Mother asked.

"Oh, I guess so," I said, not caring much one way or the other. "She always does on Saturday. Besides, she's shopping for a dress for the school dance. She'd burst if she didn't show me."

"Aren't you going to the dance?"

"No."

"Why not?"

"Didn't anyone ask you?" Keith said.

Which, in my present mood, did nothing to endear him to me. "You don't have to be asked," I said in my iciest tone. "I don't care to go."

Keith raised an eyebrow. "A little touchy this morning, aren't we? You know, denial is not a healthy way of dealing with repressed emotions."

Sometimes Keith was a pain. I toyed with the eggs on my plate and said nothing.

"Aren't you going to finish your breakfast?" Mother asked.

I set down my fork and said, "I wish we could all go back home—soon."

"You know we can't do that. We came out here primarily for the schools. Keith has to finish his education. So do you, Bernadette."

I could feel my eyes start to fill. "That's just an excuse—you don't want to go back."

"Honey, we don't know what the future will bring." She smiled teasingly. "Why, for all we know, you'll meet some handsome boy and we'll never be able to tear you away from the place."

"It's not me meeting somebody I'm worried about," I blurted out. "It's you—you and Don Justice."

Her fingers flew to stray wisps of hair and worked awkwardly at tucking them into place, the way she always did when she was uneasy. "What do you mean?"

"I mean you'll get married and we'll be stuck here forever."

She said, "Goodness, why would you think I'd marry

41

Don? I'm sure he has enough on his mind without thinking of marrying anyone." After a moment's thought she added, "Why, he has four restaurants to run. You can't imagine what a big job that is. Besides, he's been married before. He won't be anxious to make the same mistake again." She fiddled with her hair again. "Besides, my religion doesn't exactly smile on the idea of marrying someone who's been divorced."

All the time she talked, Keith stared at her intently. Finally I said, "Has he asked you?"

Her face went all red. "Of course he hasn't asked me. Goodness! You're being very silly. And I don't want to hear another word about it." She quickly got up from the table and picked up her dishes. "I'll have to rush if I'm going to make Mass this morning. Will you finish clearing up?" She started toward the kitchen but turned back. Her eyes rested on the two of us for a moment before she said, "I wish you hadn't stopped going to church." When neither of us responded, she sighed and continued on.

We both sat in silence, I pushing food around on my plate, Keith thoughtfully sipping milk. After long minutes we heard Mother's old Dodge drive off. I said, "I didn't know Mother was going to Mass this morning."

"She always goes when she's upset. You shouldn't have said what you did."

"Well, I don't want her to marry Don, do you?"

"She isn't going to marry anybody."

42

"How do you know?"

"I know she isn't."

"That's not a reason."

"I don't need a reason," he said, then fished around for one. "She isn't going to marry anyone, because she loved Dad."

"Supposing she's just tired of working and wants someone to take care of her?"

"She's got me."

"You can't take care of her. You're still in school."

"I only have a few more years."

"A few more years? I thought you were going to be a psychiatrist—that takes forever."

"I'll quit school—if it comes to that. Oh, what are you talking about? She's not going to marry anybody." He stared off into space for a moment, his blue eyes troubled. At length he said, "At least she could be true to his memory."

I realized then that he suspected the same thing I did.

"Let's forget it," he said. "I'm sure you're making too much of a perfectly natural friendship."

"I hope you're right." I relaxed a little. "Why do you suppose she said that about church?"

"I have no idea."

I eyed him curiously. "Why *did* you stop going, Keith? Because of what happened to Ralph?"

At my mention of his father, a shadow crossed Keith's

43

face. "Why are you always bringing up the accident? Why must you dwell on what's past?"

I should have known better than to mention Ralph's death. Keith always got angry whenever anyone brought up the subject. "I don't know why you're always so sensitive about it. After all, denial isn't a healthy way of dealing with repressed emotions."

Keith missed my point. "I'm not denying anything. I just don't believe in rehashing what's past."

"I'm not rehashing, I—" Oh, what was the use? I sighed. "That's not what I asked you anyhow. I asked you why you stopped going to church."

He shrugged. "I just don't believe in that stuff anymore. What about you? I thought you were going to turn Catholic when we came out here."

I sat quietly for a moment, remembering that weak attempt. Finally I said, "I tried. I really did. I had an interview with the priest at Mother's church." I suddenly felt completely forlorn. "I wanted to turn because I used to be so jealous of you and Mother and Ralph when you'd go off to church without me. I had to go to Grandmother Perry's church. I used to feel left out. When I told the priest that, he said those were the wrong reasons. He suggested that I wait until I was sure that I wasn't doing it because of others."

I could still remember what a fuss Grandmother Perry had made when Mother had converted for Ralph. Mother gave in to her about me, though. "It must be awful to be afraid of your own mother the way Mother's afraid of Grandmother Perry."

Keith gave a wry smile. "Everybody's afraid of her. Besides, the mother-daughter relationship is a complex one." I thought he was going to spout some more Freud at me, but he didn't. Instead, he shook his head. "I'm mixed up. I always thought you wanted to go to her church."

"No. Grandmother Perry said I wasn't to be confused by Popery or Romanism." Back in Willow Orchard she had picked me up every Sunday in her old but gleaming black sedan. She always checked my outfit to make sure I wore nothing to disgrace her. (No white shoes before Memorial Day or after Labor Day. It was a law, I guessed.) When she passed on me, off we'd go, prim and proper, I to Sunday school, she to church. Although I resented it at the time, in retrospect I could see that I took a certain comfort from it, too. I'd had a spiritual home. I'd belonged, without thought, without question. Not like now.

Keith said, "You've got that back-to-the-old-home-town look again."

"I was just thinking—about Sunday school. The minister's wife used to be my teacher. I remember asking her once about God—you know, who God really was."

"What did she say?"

"Nothing—right then. It took her a week. She came in with a poem about how God was love and God was

45

understanding—a lot of nice things like that. I remember it said God was the faith that came when there was no reason for faith. It was a beautiful poem. Afterward I got to thinking and wondering about how anyone could have faith if there was no reason for it. Then I went home and looked in the old Sunday-school book that used to belong to Mother. There was a picture of God—I mean, as a real person. He was awfully old and he looked mad. I didn't like him at all."

"A copy of Michaelangelo's painting?"

"Maybe." I thought about our minister in his black Sunday robe and about the priest with whom I had almost started instruction. Somehow I'd felt the same way about both of them. "You know, it's funny about priests and ministers. You get the feeling they know things they aren't telling you."

"Like what?"

"Oh—the real mysteries."

Keith's lips curled in a smile. "Keeping them all to themselves?"

"Yes. I guess it doesn't matter, though. You can learn them if you really want to."

He grinned. "You know something?"

"What?"

"You're a crazy kid."

His voice, fondly tolerant, made me feel as if I had exposed an embarrassingly sensitive part of myself.

* * *

46

By Saturday afternoon I felt a little less annoyed with the world. I had spent a busy morning in physical activity, helping Mother clean the house. After lunch I gave my own room a thorough going over. In the process I came across the notebook I had rescued in tarot class. I examined the name-and-address sticker glued to the cover. Mark Keeper. The name meant nothing to me. I went through the phone book and found a George Keeper at the same address. The boy's father, probably.

I dialed the number, and as I sat waiting for someone to answer, I riffled through the book's pages to see if there were any notes on the tarot. Instead, I found a lot of cryptic scribbles. One page had a readable name, A. Crowley, followed by some numbers. Some kind of shorthand, I supposed.

I remembered reading somewhere that anything that belonged to a person gave you power over him as long as the object was in your possession. Nail clippings and hair were especially useful, but anything would do. From my fleeting memory of the boy who had bumped me, I decided he was no one I wanted power over.

There was someone I did, though. Wilson Curtis, back in Willow Orchard. I was sure if I was back there I could take him away from Debbie. Sometimes I was so mad at her, I wanted to burn one of the black candles that was shaped in the form of a person and put a curse on her. Of course I would never do anything like that, but just thinking about it made me feel better.

Mark Keeper's phone rang and rang, but there was no answer. At that point Francine came by, so I had to give up.

There were a couple of things I really envied about Francine. For one, she was tall. I was so short, everybody mistook me for a kid. Worse, in the spots where I was flat, she poked out plenty. I also envied the fact that she was mostly raised in a French convent in Canada. That sounded so romantic. Then too, she was daring where I was a scaredy-cat. One time she even ran away from home and stayed overnight with some boys who were camping out in a backyard. She never would tell me what they'd done, though. Nothing, I'll bet.

Francine put on her new dress and modeled it for me. She wanted to show it to Keith, too, but he had already left. The thought crossed my mind that she wanted me for a friend only because she was interested in him. I hoped I was wrong, but when I told her he was working, she immediately grew restless and bored in the house. "Let's *do* something," she said.

"We could go over to the shop," I said.

"Oh, we can always go there."

"Well, what do you want to do then?"

"I don't know—something—anything." She thought about it, then said, "I know—let's go out to the witch's villa."

"Olivia Remy's place?"

"Why not?"

48

Olivia Remy lived on the Peninsula, the great hunk of hilly land south of Cerritos Beach. She had written a book about how she practiced Wicca, the old religion of the witches. After that, people began calling her the Peninsula's official witch. Although she professed to practice white magic only, Steve, Francine's stepfather, insisted she was up to her ears in Satanism.

"What do you want to go there for?" I said.

"I want to see where they hold their Black Masses. Steve says they do it all naked."

"Suppose we run into somebody?"

"So what? They're not going to be doing anything in the daytime, silly."

"I suppose not. Still—"

"Oh, come on. You never want to do anything that's fun."

So we set out, both of us in jeans and sweaters, to catch the bus in The Village, and were soon on our way to wherever the witch's villa was. Francine told the bus driver where to let us out, and in half an hour we reached our destination, one of the few roads running from the ocean boulevard up into the hills. We walked through a gated area that looked as if it once might have had a gatekeeper. A small gatehouse appeared deserted. Francine started up the road, and I followed her.

"How do you know where you're going?" I asked.

"I've heard Steve talk about it. The place is supposed to be at the end of this road."

"Steve sure knows a lot about it."

"Yeah—I wouldn't be surprised if he was a Satanist himself."

I rather doubted it. Knowing how Francine felt about him, I supposed she would have happily accused him of anything.

We must have walked for about a mile before we reached a small, Mediterranean-style house. A sign done in blue and white tiles said The Villa. In the daylight the place looked harmless and quaint.

Disappointed, we started back down the road. Then we spotted the stairs, earthen stairs with wooden risers that climbed the side of a steep hill. There must have been more than a hundred of them. From the bottom, looking up, they seemed to disappear into the sky.

"Let's see where they go," Francine said, and started up.

"I don't think we should."

She stopped and turned back to me. "Oh, come on. What harm can it do?"

I had no answer, so I said, "Oh, all right," and followed.

Up, up, up we went. Now and then a dirt landing broke the climb and we rested for a moment. For some reason I felt a little uneasy. Once something crackled in the nearby dry brush, making me start. When a lizard skittered out, then disappeared under a clump of sagebrush, I breathed a sigh of relief. We kept on climbing. By the time we reached the top, we were both huffing and puffing.

To our surprise we found a large, Doric-pillared gazebo, so Grecian in appearance it seemed more like a monument to Aphrodite than one to the demons of hell. It sat sedately at the crest and looked over a vista of rolling hills and valleys, greening from early fall rains. In the distance far below, the ocean seemed like ribbed blue glass. Although the day was clear and the sun warm, inside the gazebo I felt a chill. Suddenly a scream that sounded like a woman in mortal danger shattered the quiet.

"Oh, God," I exclaimed, terrified. "What was that?"

I was surprised to hear Francine laugh. "Silly. That's only one of the wild peacocks. They're all over this part of the Peninsula."

I breathed a sigh of relief. "You could have fooled me."

Francine sat down on one of the benches in the huge stone structure and said, "What do you bet this is where they hold their Black Masses?"

"Oh, Francine, you're crazy."

"No, I mean it. This would be an ideal place. I wonder what they use for an altar. Probably a table that they bring in and set in the middle of the gazebo. Can't you just see it? And there would have to be a sacrifice— a newborn baby most likely."

As she went on and on, describing her idea of a Black Mass, I began to imagine that the pillars were casting eerie shadows. I could easily visualize what the place would look like in moonlight with streams of pale silver turning benches, columns, and nude bodies to a ghostly pewter. I could even see the altar lit by candles, their orange flames flickering in evil, lecherous eyes.

Suddenly I had a weird premonition about this place. I sensed an evil that terrified me. At the same time a blast of cold air whipped through the gazebo. I shuddered. "Come on," I said to Francine. "Let's get out of here." Without waiting to see if she was following, I tore down the dirt stairs.

4

Keith and Giselle sat in his car outside her apartment. "Why don't you come in with me, Keith?" she said. "We can talk inside."

He readily agreed and followed her up creaky wood stairs to the second floor, flushing with pleasure to realize that she had remembered his name.

When she opened the door of her flat, the heavy, sweet smell of incense drifted out and, inside, hung oppressively on the air. Her living room held the clutter of someone more interested in ideas than in housekeeping. Books and magazines sat in piles on every table. Open shutters above a breakfast bar revealed a sink full of unwashed dishes.

Her eyes must have followed his, because she said,

"I only do my dishes once a day—much more efficient that way." She laughed as if she sensed his disapproval and thought it amusing.

Keith perched uneasily on a rattan stool at the bar while Giselle swept around the tiny kitchen, rinsing cups and heating water for coffee. Her gypsy-bright peasant blouse and long skirt looked as if they would be more at home near a campfire than next to a gas range, he thought.

"Thanks for the ride home," she said, sliding a steaming mug of instant coffee across the bar to him.

"It was the least I could do after keeping you in the store so late." He had stopped by the shop just before closing time, telling himself his father, had he been alive, would have investigated the place to be sure it was fit for a kid like Bernadette to spend so much time in.

There was one other customer in the store, a dark woman, attractive in a sensual way that for some reason repelled Keith. While Giselle started to take care of her, he made himself as unobtrusive as possible, browsing through paperbacks. Giselle spotted him anyhow and called, "Hi, there. I'm so glad you stopped by. Be with you in a minute." Then she turned back to the woman and said, "What can I do for you, Olivia?"

The woman said, "I'm all out of Love."

Keith glanced up in surprise, but Love, as it turned out, was powdered red incense. Olivia bought a large jar of it and several packs of tarot cards. "I use the

Waite deck. They're so much easier for my students to see. You did know I was giving a class in my home?"

Giselle said, "Yes, I heard."

"I'm not trying to give you competition, Giselle dear. It's more of a hobby with me, and so many of my friends have been begging me to do it for years now. I know it's taken a couple of your students, and I'm sorry about that, but some people just seem to prefer a different approach. I hope there are no hard feelings."

"Of course not," Giselle said.

After she'd left the shop, Keith said, "Interesting-looking woman."

"Yes," Giselle agreed, but her eyes brooded. "I don't know where she gets her money, but she has a big house on the Peninsula, and the tarot cards aren't all she teaches there."

"On the Peninsula? Where?" he asked.

"Have you ever noticed that old deserted gatehouse out on the boulevard?"

"Oh, sure, I know where you mean."

"Well, Olivia lives at the end of the road behind it in a place she calls The Villa. I don't really know, but some people think she's a Satanist. I doubt it, though. I do know she does past-life readings and tells fortunes. She's very good, too, I understand. Even some of the psychics consult her. As far as the kids she mentioned, there were only a few and I wasn't sorry to lose them. I had bad vibes about all of them."

Surely she was joking, he thought. But, no, her

expression was dead serious. Keith's thoughts immediately turned to Bernadette, questioning the influence of this occult environment. As if she'd read his mind, she said, "You needn't worry about your sister. She isn't interested in orgies. Her soul is pure, and I teach only things that will keep it that way."

Although he knew she was trying to reassure him, the idea still disturbed him. "Look," he said, "aren't you supposed to close at five-thirty?" When she nodded, he added, "It's after that now. I don't want to keep you, but I'd really like to talk to you about my sister. Could I give you a ride home?"

She laughed. "I live only a couple of blocks from here—but sure, if you want to."

Now here he was, taking coffee with her in her apartment, which was more than he'd hoped for. He picked up his cup and found himself frowning into the pale lipstick stain of a previous coffee drinker. He turned the cup to the other side. Hardened brown trickles accosted him. He steeled himself, then plunged ahead to take the first forlorn swallow.

Giselle lit a fat, white candle on the bar. "The candle's a symbol of the soul. I like to keep one burning."

Keith smiled absently. In a few moments, when he found he was not clutching his stomach in mortal anguish, he relaxed. "Bernadette said you had"—he glanced around cautiously—"children?"

"A boy and a girl. They're with my mother in Fullerton. They're better off there right now than in this little chicken coop."

Keith nodded soberly, trying to appear sympathetic. He'd been hoping Bernadette had lied.

"Now what about your sister?"

"My sister? Oh, yes . . ."

"In the shop you said you wanted to talk about her."

"Oh, I do." Then he paused, wondering how he could broach the subject without offending her. Finally, he said, "She's really my stepsister."

"Oh? I didn't know."

"Oh, yes." He nodded as if the revelation had some startling significance she might care to ponder while he went on searching his mind for the correct way to handle the topic. At last he said, "This fortune-telling stuff . . ." He stared beyond Giselle, then found himself focusing on the pile of dirty dishes. He averted his eyes and picked up his cup for a swig of coffee. When the half-moon of lipstick met him partway, second thoughts prevailed and the cup found its way back to the bar.

In a fatherly voice now he said, "I don't think learning to tell fortunes is good for Bernadette." He shook his head very slowly, hoping to give her the impression that he had been reflecting seriously on the matter. "Tell me something—you don't really believe in any of this stuff, do you?"

"Of course I do. Great Zot, I wouldn't teach it if I didn't!" She smiled, and Keith began losing himself in her dimples. "I'll bet you don't know the first thing about the tarot."

"No, I guess I don't."

Giselle got up and, in the living room, took a small box from a table drawer. She returned to the bar, pulled a deck of cards from the box, and handed it to Keith. "Okay," she said. "We'll just do something simple. Shuffle the cards three times and ask something that can be answered yes or no. Then cut them in thirds."

Feeling embarrassed, he did as she asked, pushing the offensive cup far out of the way. "Am I supposed to tell you what I asked?"

"It will help me read the cards."

"All right. I asked if I should become a psychiatrist. But I think you should know that I don't believe in this kind of thing."

She answered him with a smile, then picked up the cards and laid out five. After studying them, she said, "The cards say, maybe. At least, the way things are going right now, you'd better give it more thought."

Keith frowned. "Are you sure you're reading them right?"

"Oh, yes." She pointed to one on her right. "This is the past. The card represents prudent, loving guidance—someone out of your past who was close to you and cared about you."

"My father," Keith said without hesitation. Surprised by his own ready gullibility, he ran a hand over the dark

58

shadow of his beard, hoping the act would hide his pink face.

"The next one is in the past, too, an unexpected happening, something you didn't want—something that happened to him."

Keith's eyes fixed on the cards with fascinated horror. "He was killed. . . ."

Giselle looked up. "Oh, I'm sorry." Her eyes grew soft with compassion. "The accident was in a building, wasn't it?"

He glanced at her sharply. "How did you know that— my sister?"

"I don't know," she said, her voice distant. "It was an image that suddenly filled my head. Maybe Bernadette did mention it, although I don't think so."

"Yes, it was in a building—one he was putting up. He was a contractor. An I-beam fell on him."

"Want to tell me about it?"

He stiffened. "I really don't want to talk about it."

"Don't want to—or can't?"

He shrugged coldly.

Giselle said nothing. When her silence lengthened uncomfortably, he felt he had to fill it, and words began to trickle out. "We were supposed to meet with my counselor at school that afternoon. The three of us— my stepmother, Louise, Dad, and I—we all had to go. I can't even remember what it was about, but we had to pick Dad up on the job." He paused, remembering

59

fondly how his dad could never be around a job without pitching in.

The words were hard to get out, but he continued. "I reminded Louise that he'd be dirty. She was a little late anyhow, but she ran back into the house for a clean shirt. And that was all it took—those few extra minutes—that damned shirt." The memory that he always tried so hard to block from his mind filled his head now: Louise waiting in the car, he scurrying along toward the skeleton of the hotel his dad was building, the crane lifting an I-beam, his dad shouting something to someone on the ground, never seeing the crane accidentally release the beam, and Keith frozen in horror, shrieking, "Look out, Dad, look out!"

Giselle brought him back to the present. "Do you feel it was your stepmother's fault—because she was late?"

"Of course not," he said, appalled.

"Yours then—for reminding her about the shirt?"

He felt his jaw tighten. "It wasn't anyone's fault. It just happened." He closed his mouth to drop the subject, then just couldn't let it go. "Why, you might just as well blame my teacher for asking us to meet with her that afternoon. Of course it wasn't my fault. Why would you even suggest such a thing?"

"I wasn't suggesting anything, Keith. It was just that you had a certain look on your face that made me wonder if you felt somehow guilty."

"Oh, no. You're way off—way off."

"Okay," she said agreeably.

He was amazed that he'd told her so much. Usually he couldn't talk about the accident at all, never even let himself think about it. He felt that she had somehow bewitched the words right out of him, and the thought angered him. "I think we should change the subject."

Her eyes glinted with amusement. "I know—mind my own business."

Now he regretted his words. "I didn't really mean it that way. It's nice of you to take an interest." He glanced back to the cards. "What else do those things say?"

Giselle pointed to the center card. "This represents you and the realization of your wish, but it's turned upside down."

"What does that mean?"

"With the other cards, it means there's something unsettled in your mind about becoming a psychiatrist."

Keith nodded. "And the last two?"

"A dark man and a fair woman. They figure in the future, and their relationship has a great deal to do with your question."

"Louise and Don," Keith murmured, half to himself. "Don?"

"Louise's boss at El Bandido." If he quit school and got a job, there would be no reason for Louise to work, he had decided. A good paycheck would remove her from the designs of all the marriage-minded men Keith was sure were lurking in business establishments all over the Los Angeles area, waiting to propose to Louise and take her reluctant family to their bosoms.

He frowned down at the cards. "You know, I don't believe any of this stuff"—his index finger swept across the fairy-tale drawings of the tarot—"and yet it's really uncanny." He sat for a moment, mulling over its amazing accuracy. Then a light dawned. "Now, wait a minute—can you do this again, asking the same question?"

"Sure." Giselle went through the same thing a second time. Again the cards said maybe. Again each, in one way or another, related to the problem.

"I see," he said, trying not to sound too superior. "You realize what I'm doing, of course."

"What's that?"

"I'm reading my own thoughts into the cards, interpreting—no, juggling meanings to fit the situation as I see it. It's all association, something like a Rorschach test."

"That's what it's all about."

He stared at her curiously.

"You read the cards at your own level of awareness," she said with the smile of a teacher pleased with her pupil. "Your soul already holds the key to your future. This is a way of getting in touch with your soul."

"Your id, you mean."

"I mean soul."

Keith laughed. "All right—soul. It's therapy then—self-therapy."

"In a way."

"I suppose it's not so bad then—just a way of puzzling over your problems. What if the cards had said yes the second time?"

"It would have meant you'd gained some new insight, perhaps from the first reading, and it would make it okay to go ahead with your plans now."

Keith gave it some thought. "If you took out the yes and no stuff, this kind of thing could have therapeutic value—might even do some good."

"That's what I like about the cards. You see, when you read cards, it's just between you and your soul—nothing in between."

"Yes, I can see that," he said agreeably.

"When people fool around with crystal balls and automatic writing, they're really asking for it. All you get are low spirits that way. And they'll tell you anything, because they don't know any more than you do."

Keith stared at her. For an instant his mind tracked the whole progress of human life, from magic to religion to science, and in the intense expression in her eyes found its way back to magic. How could someone on her apparent intellectual level regress to concepts so primitive? Feeling his way, he said, "Are you—do you go to church?"

"I'm a Catholic." Her eyes were serious. "I go to Mass on Sundays; then I go to the Church of Religious Science, which I like too. So you see, spiritually I'm very well taken care of."

"But how do you reconcile one with the other? I mean, your church—or churches—with occultism?"

"I don't like the word *occult*. That's as bad as calling someone a food faddist. People interested in good nutrition aren't faddists. And as far as religion goes, for me, there's no conflict. I'm . . ." She shrugged. "I'm very satisfied. How about you?"

"I'm—well, I used to be a Catholic."

"What are you now?"

"I'm not anything now."

She cocked her head. "Why? Because your father was killed?"

"That has nothing to do with it," he said shortly, then realized that he must sound as if he were protesting too much. He glanced at her to find her watching him, a curious expression on her face. "Well, maybe it has something to do with it, but it would have happened anyhow."

When she said nothing, he added, "Well, how is someone supposed to react when something like that happens? What are you supposed to tell yourself? It was God's will? It only wakes you up. In one second the life of my father, a good guy, was taken for no reason. For no reason!" He glared unseeing at the tarot cards. "No, you can't tell me there's some Great Father out there in the ether—watching—caring. There's only yourself—all alone."

"And lonely?"

"Maybe." He had never spilled out so much of himself before. "You *must* have some kind of magic to get that much out of me." He smiled awkwardly. "Are you going to try to convert me?"

Her eyebrows lifted. "No, I don't think so. There's really no need. In the end, loneliness always turns toward something—or someone. Everyone has to believe that something is sacred."

"Or someone?" His eyes met hers. At that moment he would have happily put her in that exalted position.

But she turned away. "How old are you, Keith?"

The gossamer thread that had connected them for a moment broke. He looked down at the bar and at his long, bony hands clasped tight in front of him. "What does that have to do with anything?"

"How old?" she persisted.

He felt himself blush like a kid. "Almost twenty."

"I'm twenty-six."

He contained a sigh of relief. "That's hardly any difference at all."

"Seven long years."

"More like six." He grinned. "If I promise to try to catch up, can we be friends?"

She laughed, and her dimples, her enchanting dimples, came into play again. "Of course we can be friends." She got up and headed for the kettle on the stove. "Now, how about some more hot coffee?"

He pulled his nearly full cup toward him. "This is

enough, thanks." He found the lipstick stain—hers, he hoped—and pressed it against his lips as he drained the cup. "I suppose I should really get going. I have a chemistry exam tomorrow. Can I take a rain check on that coffee?"

"Sure. Anytime."

He lingered at her door, drawing out his good-bye to give her every chance to notice how he towered above her. "Well, I guess I'd better be going," he said again, and started down the stairs. He nearly bumped into a big brute of a man who moved around Keith to continue his lumbering climb.

"Hey, Giselle!" the brute called when he spotted her, still on the landing. "Y'know that scarab ring of the landlady's, the one she thought was cursed?"

Keith's steps slowed. He turned around and glanced up the stairs. The big guy joined Giselle and said, "I held that ring in my hand, and I didn't get nothin' but good vibrations."

"That's super, Sammy," Giselle said.

Keith waited until their voices faded into the apartment, feeling all the resentment of a jealous child. A moment's thought brought him to his senses. Giselle had to be too discriminating to go for some fat gorilla. With that comforting notion, he tripped lightly down the remaining stairs, glided out the front door, slid into his car, and *vroom*ed off.

66

5

Two weeks had passed since Francine and I had visited that strange site at Olivia Remy's villa. Every time I thought of that afternoon, I felt again the same chill I had experienced there. I chided myself for having too much imagination.

During that period I carried Mark Keeper's notebook to the Wednesday-night tarot classes, but he never showed. I decided that he'd probably quit the course, but I'd better try again to reach him by phone.

Often I took out the pentagram I'd made and just stared at it, wondering why it wasn't working faster. I hadn't tried standing within the circle again and conjuring up Astaroth, because the act was so dangerous. Once should have been enough. I told myself I had only to be patient.

In the meantime, there were other things I could do. I had even been concentrating extra hard on my Wheel of Fortune, something Francine had showed me how to make. You draw a great big circle on heavy paper, then divide it into wedges like a pie. Each wedge is for something you want. You write in it and find magazine pictures that represent the wish. You have to be very exact about what you want, and writing it down and making a picture of it on paper help to strengthen the image in your mind. Then, when you know what you want, you can start willing it to happen.

I had a beautiful wedge for Willow Orchard, with pictures of green trees and houses—one that reminded me of Grandmother Perry's, all gingerbread—and even pictures of streetlights that looked almost like the ones there. I had another wedge for Don Justice. I'd cut out a picture of a man who looked a little like him and printed Don's name below. In the same wedge I'd pasted a magazine drawing of a nice-looking mature woman with black hair, one whom no one could mistake for Mother. I called her *Wonderful new woman in Don Justice's life.* Even with all my concentration, I couldn't see that anything was changing.

In fact, nothing seemed to be going right. For instance, there was the car incident. One night the VW broke down completely. Keith had to call one of his school friends to come and help him push it to a garage. When Mother found out it would take about two hundred dollars to repair it, she unfortunately had to tell Don, who couldn't resist putting in his two cents' worth. Don told Mother that what Keith needed, although he probably didn't realize it, was not exotic foreign design but good old American reliability.

Keith really blew his top. "What does he know about it?" he yelled at Mother. "I doubt if he knows anything about cars. What are you asking *him* for, anyhow? It's my car—ask me!"

Mother said, "He was only trying to help, Keith. Besides, I think he's right. You've had nothing but trouble with that car since you bought it."

"Of course he's right," Keith said. "Everybody's right except me. It doesn't matter what *I* want—all that matters is what *he* wants."

Then he apologized for yelling, but I understood how he felt. Who wanted Don running our lives? In the end, Mother backed down and let him borrow the money from her. He was to repay it in installments from his store earnings. The car was behaving properly now, but Keith was not.

At times he seemed very high, then at other times he was so grouchy it was hard to be around him. And he was out late just about every night, and I was sure he hadn't had any work calls. Although I wasn't about to tell on him, I knew Mother wouldn't like it at all. She didn't want me staying alone until the late hour that she came home.

One Friday night, after Mother went to work and Keith was off to wherever he was off to, I started going through some things in my room when I came across the notebook I'd picked up in tarot class. I decided to try phoning again. I went out to the kitchen, where our only telephone was, looked up the number, and dialed. To my surprise, this time someone said hello, and the voice sounded young and male.

"May I speak to Mark Keeper, please," I said.

He sounded suspicious as he asked, "What do you want to speak to me about?"

"Oh, are you him? I didn't realize. Look, you don't know me but I'm the one you bumped into in that tarot class we're taking. At least, *I'm* taking it. I haven't seen you there lately, so I guess you're not taking it anymore, but I just thought you'd like to know that you dropped a notebook there and I picked it up. If you're coming next Wednesday, I'll bring it."

"*You* found it! How come you waited so long to let me know?" He really sounded mad.

"I'm sorry. I did take it to class, but you weren't there. And I did try to call, but no one was home. And then I guess I just forgot all about it. I really am sorry."

There was a long silence. Finally he said, "Tell me where you live and I'll come get it now."

"Oh, not now," I said quickly.

"Why not?"

I was about to say *because I'm home all alone*, but I

caught myself. Mother said you never told people that. "It just isn't convenient now. If you want to stop by tomorrow afternoon, it will be all right. If I'm not here, I'll leave it with my mother."

"Oh . . ." There was another long silence. At length he said, "Well, okay. Give me your address."

I told him where we lived and hung up. Then my thoughts returned to my pentagram. I decided that I'd have to try conjuring up Astaroth again, and this time be more demanding. So, once more, I stood within the circle and commanded him to appear, threatening him with the Holy Angels of Heaven and the Mighty Wisdom of God. This time I received no sign, yet I still had the feeling that my words were heard. Again I told him what I wanted, then used the incantation to send him back to darkness.

I had no sooner finished when the phone rang. It was Francine. She had been home with a strep throat for the past couple of weeks, so I hadn't seen her since that scary experience in the gazebo.

Francine said, "I had a terrible fight with my mother, so I just left."

"Left? Like in running away or something?"

"Mostly something."

"What does that mean?"

"It doesn't mean much of anything, I guess. But I had to do something. They—Steve and her—they treat me like a maid. It's just not right. I do all the housecleaning—all of it, and every night I put dinner on. Sure, Mom tells me what to fix and how to do it, but the job always falls on me, because they're in the shop so much. And after dinner I do all the cleaning up, because they both have other things to do. Well, tonight Steve just went one step too far, and I blew up."

"What did he do?"

"He comes out of his bedroom with all his dirty laundry and says, 'Francine, how about running these through the washer and dryer for me. I'm teaching a class tonight, and your mother has to work in the shop.' Then he hands me all his stuff and says, 'If you take the shirts out of the dryer as soon as it stops, you won't have to press them.' Can you believe that?"

I could sympathize with her. No one minds doing some chores, but I knew Francine did everything in that house, and the more she did, the more they seemed to pile on her. "What did you say to him?" I asked.

"Nothing—not to him. I waited until he was out of the house, then I blew up. I told Mom, 'I'm just not doing that man's laundry. I do enough as it is. If I'm going to be the housekeeper around here, then I think I should get a housekeeper's wages and not just a paltry allowance.' Mom says, 'Oh, come on, Francine. He really needs those clothes tomorrow. It won't kill you to do it once.' 'Once!' I say. 'Are you kidding? Once means from now on. No, Mom, I just won't do it, and knowing the way I feel about him, I think he's got a big nerve to ask.' "

"What did she say?"

"I didn't give her a chance to say anything. I walked over and handed her the whole pile. 'He's your husband, not mine,' I said, and turned around and walked out."

"Wow!"

"Wow is right. But I don't think I'm being unreasonable, do you?"

"Not with all *you* do around that place. I guess you just had to take a stand."

"That's it—that's exactly it. I had to take a stand. I walked out because I wanted Mom to have some time to think about it by herself."

As far as I was concerned, Eva and Steve did treat Francine like a drudge. I couldn't blame her for finally rebelling. "I guess you did the wisest thing. What are you going to do while you're making her suffer?"

"I don't know. I thought maybe you could meet me in The Village, and we could go someplace and find something interesting to do."

"You know my mother doesn't want me running around like that at night."

"She doesn't have to know. She's working, isn't she? And Keith's out, so he won't know."

"Keith—how did you know he wasn't here?"

"Because, dear friend, just about ten minutes ago I saw his car in front of Giselle's apartment. And I doubt very much he was visiting Sammy Rupp."

Giselle? Did that explain what he was doing nights?

I said, "There are other people who live in that apartment house besides Giselle and Sammy, you know. Keith is most likely visiting one of his friends from college."

"I doubt it. But that's neither here nor there. I don't want to go home until late—give them something to worry about. How about meeting me? We can have some fun—maybe even go up to the Strip. I've always wanted to do that."

"Sunset Strip? You're crazy, Francine. How do you think you're going to get there? Hitching rides?"

"Why not? Or we could go down to Olivia's. She has her tarot class on Friday nights. Might be interesting."

"Oh, Francine, your mother would be so mad at you—"

"Who cares about my mother? All she ever thinks about is that stupid wrestler she's married to."

I knew she didn't mean that. She was just mad. I said, "Look, Francine, you know you're just talking. You wouldn't really try to go to either of those places."

"Oh, wouldn't I?"

"No, you wouldn't. Why don't you just come over here? We can make some popcorn and watch television."

"Oh, big deal."

"Come on, Francine. You know your mother wouldn't want you running around at night all by yourself."

She sighed, then said, "Oh, well—I may come over

later. I'm not promising now—but I may. First, though, there's something else I think I'll do."

"What?"

"I'll tell you about it if I see you later."

After I hung up, I wasn't even curious. Francine loved making any piddling thing she did sound mysterious and important. I took an orange soda from the refrigerator, opened it, and swigged from the bottle. Delicious. I decided to make some popcorn whether or not Francine stopped by, so I got out the popper and soon had a big bowl full of the stuff. The house smelled just wonderful.

As I took it into the living room, planning to turn on the television set, the doorbell rang. We always kept the porch light burning at night, so I peeked out the front window and recognized the boy I'd just called about his notebook. I had told him to come tomorrow. He must have misunderstood. I knew Mother didn't want me to let strangers into the house, but this was different. He wasn't exactly a stranger, and I *had* called him. Besides, I knew what he wanted—his old notebook. I might just as well give it to him and be done with it.

When I opened the door, a cold, gusty wind swept across the porch, setting his long hair flying. He brushed it out of his eyes and said, "I came for my book—somebody called me."

"I did," I said, then couldn't resist adding, "You were supposed to come tomorrow, not tonight."

"Yeah—well—I just found out I couldn't make it tomorrow, so I thought I'd better drive right over and get it now."

I looked beyond him to the curb, where some kind of compact car was parked. If he was already driving, he had to be at least sixteen, yet I wouldn't have guessed it. Although he was tall, he had a frail, stooped look that somehow made him look much younger.

"I'll get your notebook," I said, and another blast of wind tore over the porch and into the house. I wanted to close the door in his face, but that seemed so rude. "If you want to get out of the wind, you can wait inside."

He ran his fingers through his now-unkempt hair, trying to smooth it back into place. "Thanks," he said, and stepped through the doorway, which opened directly into the living room.

I closed the door quickly against the wind. "I'll get your book right away." Then I realized I was still holding the bottle of orange soda. There was no handy place to set it down without leaving a ring on the furniture, so I hurried out to the kitchen and put it on the counter. Before I could make for my room, Grit came flying through the cat door that Keith had so patiently installed. Old Grit could come and go as he pleased, but he was never so far away he couldn't hear kitchen activity. He knew that usually meant an extra snack for him.

"Not now, Grit," I said, and hastily went on to my

bedroom to retrieve the notebook. Then I headed back to the living room, looking forward to getting rid of Mark Keeper and settling down to my popcorn and television.

As I entered the room, I expected to see him standing in the spot where I'd left him. Instead, he was stiffly seated on the edge of the couch. Before I realized what was happening, Grit bounded across the room and, with one graceful leap, landed smartly in the middle of Mark's lap.

In the next instant a bloodcurdling shriek rang through the house. As if a bomb had exploded beneath him, Mark shot to his feet, and Grit went sailing across the room to disappear into the kitchen. I heard the clap of the rubber cat door and knew that Grit had disappeared into the night.

Stunned and at a loss, I stood rooted to my spot near the door. I'd heard of people who were phobic about cats, but I'd never really met one before. Finally, I gingerly made my way over to Mark, afraid I might startle him into another awful shriek. "Did he scare you?" I asked stupidly.

He gawked at me in silence, his face ashen, his body trembling all over. I don't know how long we stood staring at each other, perhaps only seconds, before he said, "I'm going to be sick."

Frantically, I stabbed a finger toward the hallway. "In there. First door to your right."

He tore off in the direction I'd pointed, and I sank down into the nearest chair, my own stomach feeling queasy now. All I could visualize was vomit all over the floor of the bathroom and my having to clean it up. To my relief, after a few moments passed, I heard the flush of the toilet. Apparently he'd made it in time.

Seconds later I turned around to find Mark peering around the hall door. "Is it gone?" he asked.

I had to feel sorry for him. His face was chalky white, and his dark, disheveled hair hung limply around his cheeks. He looked ready to collapse. "You don't have to worry about Grit. He's gone for the night. You scared him as much as he scared you."

He came into the room and, as if he didn't trust his legs, sank into a chair. "I'm sorry. I have a thing about cats—I can't help it." He gave me a defensive look. "Some people can't, you know."

"I know."

"My father says I'm nuts."

"Why would he say a thing like that? Lots of people are phobic about something. I'm afraid of high places myself. I'll bet even he's afraid of something."

"Aw, him—the only thing he's afraid of is God."

Obviously he didn't like his father very much. I really didn't know what to say to him, so of course I said the wrong thing. "I'll bet your mother understands."

"My mother's dead." He must have been bordering on tears, because now they spilled over and ran down his cheeks.

I felt terrible. Again I didn't know what to say, so this time I said nothing.

After a time he wiped his eyes on the sleeves of his jacket, sniffled, then said, "I'm sorry. It's just that we were pretty close, my mother and me."

I kept wishing he would get up and leave, but I couldn't say anything. I still wasn't sure he felt well enough to drive. Although I didn't want to hear it, he started pouring out his sad story, almost as if being sick in front of me had somehow shattered his defenses. Or as if having purged himself physically, he now had to purge himself emotionally. The only thing I could do was listen.

Until two years ago, it seemed, his mother had protected him from a father who sounded like a tyrant even though the man spent all of his free time working for his church.

"He's always gone," Mark said. "Always doing his good works. Well, he never did anything good for me and my mother—especially not for me." He shrugged hopelessly. "Well, it doesn't make any difference. Nothing ever goes right for me anyhow. Never did— never will."

"Nothing?" I asked.

"Nothing. Not one stinking thing. I never once got anything I wanted that it didn't turn out all wrong. I just have to touch something and it turns to—" He broke off. "Well, you know what I mean."

His words made me think of the story Sammy Rupp

had once told me about himself. Without thinking, I said, "You sound just like Sammy Rupp when he was hexed. Do you know Sammy?"

He stared at me curiously. "I know who he is, but I don't know anything about him. What do you mean, he was hexed?" He leaned forward in his seat.

Now that I'd brought up the subject, I felt I had to continue. "It was back in Pennsylvania before he went into the service. He says everything went wrong for him. Just everything. He had no money and he was sick and things just got worse and worse. He says he knew some witch had put a hex on him, but he never could find out who. If you know who it is, you can do something about it. He never did find out either, but what happened to him was just like a miracle.

"He was sent to Vietnam, and in his very first battle he was shot. They left him for dead, Sammy says. He thinks he probably did die for a time. When they took him to the hospital, he revived and they put a steel plate in his head. Ever since that time he's been psychic— and the hex is gone. Sammy thinks that dying freed him from whoever had power over him." I didn't really believe that Sammy had died, but he *did* have a steel plate in his head. Everyone said so. And he was good at predicting the future.

Mark was really leaning forward in his chair now. "I never heard that about him."

"It's true. At least that's what Sammy believes."

He nodded thoughtfully. "For a long time now I've had the feeling that someone was out to get me. I even consulted somebody about it, somebody who really knows about things like that. All she'd say was that someone wished me ill. She wouldn't tell me who it was, though, said she didn't know. But I don't believe her. I got it figured out that the reason she won't tell me is because it's someone she knows, someone who consults her too. She says all her consultations are strictly confidential."

Someone wished him ill? That sounded like fortune-teller talk. "Maybe Sammy could find out."

I was relieved to see the color coming back to Mark's face. Obviously I'd given him something to hang on to. He did look like someone who'd been hexed, I thought. However, now that he no longer seemed sick, all I wanted was to see him go. The sound of a car driving by reminded me of Keith. If he ever walked in on us, I'd never hear the end of it. "My brother will be home any minute," I said. "I'm not supposed to have anyone in the house when no one's here."

He glanced around the room, looking as if, up to now, he hadn't realized we were alone. I stood up and he took the hint. "Well, I guess I'd better be going," he said. "But thanks for all that information. That was interesting."

After he'd left, I breathed a sign of relief. I decided that if anyone was hexed, it had to be Mark Keeper.

6

Since Keith's first visit to Giselle's apartment he had been dropping in regularly, at first using any excuse that came to mind. She'd finally said to him, "You don't need an excuse to come here. I love company."

That was the trouble. He seldom had her to himself. On the few occasions when he did, they discussed life and love and themselves, which gave him what felt like a small taste of heaven. Unfortunately, though, those were rare evenings. The rest of the time he found himself more and more disgruntled.

On the same night that Bernadette was advising Mark Keeper, Keith had walked in on Giselle as she stood in the middle of the living-room floor, a piece of jewelry pressed against her brow, a study in concentration. As usual the door was ajar, an invitation for everyone and his brother to stop in.

There was never any privacy, Keith thought. Everyone in the building roamed in and out at will. Giselle loved them all, from the young girl who shared an apartment with about twenty friends, male and female, to the bachelor who carried a black rat with him everyplace he went, to Sammy, the chubby psychic. More than once Keith had found Giselle and Sammy, heads together, bent over a crystal ball or over the idiotic fortune-telling cards, but this was the first time he had found her like this, unaware of even the sound of the closing door.

He stood for a moment staring at her. He had a headache, one that he was sure was psychosomatic, caused by the frustration of never knowing where he stood with her. Tonight, though, he was determined to find out. "What are you up to now?" he asked, feeling irritable.

"Oh, Keith . . ." She turned and smiled at him, showing the big dimples that never failed to disarm him. He noticed she was wearing the beauty mark she always wore for entertaining. Before he could ask where she was headed, she held out the bracelet that had been at her forehead. "Isn't it lovely? I bought it in an antiques shop."

"What were you doing with it just now?"

"Psychometry. That's sort of a clairvoyant free

83

association. I was trying to see what vibrations I could get from it, see if I could tell what kind of person had owned it."

Keith refused to pursue the subject of vibrations. He was sick of vibrations and annoyed at having to share Giselle with another world so closed to him. He had no feeling of security in their relationship, as platonic as she managed to keep it. He was always afraid the cards would decide against him. Whenever she was unavailable, he never knew whether he could believe the simple reason she gave or whether she was covering up for some disastrous warning that had come from the tarot. More than once she'd said that when she had psychic qualms about an engagement to entertain at a party, she found excuses to skip it. She was so guided by imaginary forces that he felt helpless beside them.

There were times when he thought she was absolutely perfect. When he was annoyed with her, he could see only her faults. She kept great piles of books and magazines around because she couldn't bear to part with anything with print on it until she'd read it. And she seldom had a chance to read, so her apartment always looked messy. Not only that, she had no sense of time and was constantly late for appointments. He kept a long list of Giselle's faults in a special compartment in his head and enjoyed pulling it out when he was angry with her, as he was tonight.

"Come and sit down," she said now, patting the seat

of a chair facing the divan on which she seated herself. "You can only stay a little while. I have a party tonight."

"Don't go."

She looked at him with amused tolerance. "They're counting on me. Besides, I need the money. And *you* could use a little time for study."

"Then let me drive you and pick you up. It's not safe for women to drive around alone at night."

She laughed. "Oh, Keith, that's so sweet of you, but you know it won't work. I can't tell what time I'll get through. It's much simpler to take my own car. Now don't look so put out. You know I'm right. Besides, I always drive with both doors locked."

"I don't like to think of you at parties with a bunch of drunks. I'll bet they make passes at you."

"Not anymore. Not since I've been going to the classes Steve gives." When she saw his blank look, she added, "You know—Francine's stepfather. He gives ESP classes. One of the things he's been teaching is how to control other people with the use of hand motions. It's wonderful—really. No one knows what I'm doing, but with the gestures I make, I can keep people away from me."

There it was again. There was no escaping the psychic world. He felt it was consuming her. On the few occasions when he had tried to talk to her about it, he had been interrupted. Someone was always popping in.

As nearly as Keith could figure out, Giselle believed humans were little pieces of God, broken away. They were God and the universe in miniature. Her idea was to develop the divine spark within her to gain mastery over the universe and ultimately reunite herself with God. In some ways her thinking leaned toward the Gnostic, she said, explaining that *gnosis* meant the knowledge of God.

"How do you intend to develop this divine spark?" he'd once asked her, trying to keep the sarcasm out of his voice.

"Not the way someone like you would go about it. The knowledge of God can't be gained by proof, or by arguing about the nature of God, or by any rational means. It can only be found through direct divine inspiration or through the sacred traditions, which were divinely inspired. The secret knowledge is there—much of it in books like the Cabala. To learn it is to know God. To know God is to be God."

She was fanatically devout in the truths she said had been revealed over the ages through mediums.

"And just what is it mediums are supposed to have revealed?" he had asked her.

"Knowledge of the spiritual world. That's only a theory though. But it may well be the way it was done, because in more recent times there have been cases of noted people coming back through mediums and telling what it's like after death and what the universe is all about."

"And what is it all about—according to these people?"

"Well, no matter how they express it, essentially it seems to agree with the Cabala. It—how can I tell you? To start with, God *is* the universe, the total of all things." She spoke with great intensity, almost in a trance. "In the beginning there was God and nothing. God sent out emanations from himself, ten of them, into the nothing. We call them lights. In the Cabala, they're the *sephiroth*—numbers or categories. They're arranged in layers, like the skin of an onion. The outer skin is the sphere of God. Within this are spheres of stars, spheres for each of the planets, until you get to the moon and earth.

"The soul comes from God to be imprisoned in a human body, but it wants to get back to God—wants that very much. To get back, it must climb through the spheres to heaven. But the spheres are guarded by angels and devils who will try to turn it back unless it has been initiated in the secret traditions. You might say it's like learning passwords that make the gates open to let the soul continue on its way to God."

"You mean," Keith said, "all I have to do is learn what's in these books and I'll be assured safe passage to God after death?"

"Even in life, some people believe."

"What about goodness, morality? Doesn't that have anything to do with it? So far, the ticket only mentions knowledge."

"I know," Giselle said. "And that's what the black magician believes, that it's not morality but ignorance that separates humans from God. I can't quite go along with that."

"If you think all these truths were passed from the beyond to mediums, psychologists would disagree with you. They think the little spirits who talk through mediums are merely secondary personalities of the mediums."

"Oh, psychologists," Giselle said with a scoffing tone.

Anything she disliked hearing she ignored, he felt. He added, "My beliefs aren't so different from yours. I believe the entire cosmos consists of the same world stuff. I don't care what name you give it. And I believe education and knowledge are the most important qualities people can strive for, but not in your way. Haven't you read Julian Huxley? All knowledge should be tested against fact, he says. Truth isn't something that somebody revealed once and for all; truth is something that has to be progressively discovered."

She said nothing.

Keith went on. "Science believes the limits of physiological efficiency have been reached by life, and the only creatures capable of further advancement are humans—through the brain and the mind. Whether we like it or not, we're now the main agents for the evolution of the earth and its dwellers. And this is our destiny—realizing our own possibilities, not wasting ourselves soaking up a lot of supernatural gibberish."

He continued arguing for reason, but there was no moving her. The more she exposed her mind to him, the less he was able to reach her. And the less he was able to reach her, the stronger his need to reform her grew.

Now as he watched her clasp the bracelet to her wrist, he said, "There are natural explanations for all your occult beliefs. If you've learned body language to repel men at parties and are consciously using it, then you're probably unconsciously making yourself seem aloof. That would certainly put a guy off."

Before she could respond, there was a light tap at the door and Giselle called, "Enter."

The door opened, and Francine's gleaming blond head appeared. She glanced over to Keith and said, "Oh, I didn't realize you had company. Maybe I should come back another time."

Keith silently groaned.

Giselle said, "Don't be silly, Francine. Keith isn't company. Come on in."

Francine seemed to prance in. She removed her jacket and tossed it over a chair back. Then she took one look around the cluttered room, chose a spot near the coffee table, and even in tight jeans managed to squat, yogi fashion, on the floor. She toyed with the items on the table until she found matches to light the powdered incense waiting in a metal urn. A sickeningly sweet smell filled Keith's nostrils.

He must have made a face, because Giselle said, "Keith doesn't like incense."

"It's okay," he said. It was too late anyhow. The stuff was already burning.

"Oh, I'm so sorry. I didn't know." Francine flashed him the kind of smile that, he supposed, was meant to be madly alluring. Her adolescent libido was certainly wasted on him.

"What's up, Francine?" Giselle asked.

Francine had a long tale of woe about how badly she was treated at home, which, to Keith's thinking, all boiled down to some silly story about her mother's having expected Francine to do some laundry, or some such thing.

"She expects me to be a slave to her and Steve," she said. "I have to do all the housecleaning and put on dinner every night so it'll be ready when they come home. It's too much. And now Steve expects me to start washing his dirty clothes. Well, I just won't do it. They both think they can get away with anything with me. They think there's nothing I can do about it—but they're wrong."

Keith's head began to pound again. Francine probably wasn't any more impossible than any other kid her age, but tonight, especially, he had no patience with her. All he could do was tune her out and return his thoughts to Giselle and the hand motions. Was she using them on him? he wondered. Not that it would have worked in quite the way she intended, but was that what he sensed when he tried to get close to her? Was she holding him off—mentally perhaps? And was he some kind of masochist that he needed to be treated badly?

When his attention returned to the present, Giselle was saying, "Now, don't get excited, Francine. I know you have to do an awful lot around the house, but your mother says it's only until the store shows more of a profit. Eva's good to you in other ways, and you know it. Everyone feels hassled by their parents once in a while. Tomorrow everything will seem different."

"Sure, Francine," Keith put in wearily. "I'll bet if you went right home now, you'd find your mother was all over it—probably sorry she even blew up."

"Ha!" Francine said. "You don't know my mother," and showed no indication of going anywhere.

She was exasperating, Keith thought. Why in God's name hadn't she done what she was told in the first place? Then she'd be at home where she belonged. With her here, how was he ever going to have a chance to talk to Giselle? And he *had* to talk to her. Perhaps it was the age difference. Seven years. That might seem insurmountable to her. Not to him, though. Age was not measured in years but in maturity. Since the death of his father, he had aged ten years, he was sure. And he looked older than he was, while Giselle looked years younger than twenty-six. Intellectually he was more mature, too. And wiser.

Giselle said, "What are you going to do, Francine?

91

You can't stay here too long. I have to entertain at a party tonight."

"Don't worry, I wasn't planning on staying here," Francine said.

Keith thought, Thank God for small mercies. She couldn't leave soon enough to please him. He had so much to get off his mind. Things that had to be said. Would he have the nerve to say them to Giselle? Or would he back down as he usually did, worried that if he unburdened himself, it would bring an end to everything, to all the evenings he spent with her? Even though he seldom had her to himself.

Perhaps it wasn't the age difference, after all. Perhaps she found him awkward. He had never been seriously involved with a girl before. Maybe he was doing everything wrong. Or maybe she was comparing him to her ex-husband, who was probably the masterful type. On the other hand, he'd heard her say that she and her ex just couldn't make it. Or was it something about sun signs? She had asked what his was soon after they'd met. Yes, that could well be the reason. She believed all that zodiac stuff. Most likely his Taurus was incompatible with her Sagittarius.

"Perhaps you could go over and see Bernadette until you cool off," Giselle suggested to Francine.

Francine gave a sly smile. "You don't have to worry about me. I have my own plans."

"What kind of plans?"

Francine shrugged. "There are plenty of places to go if you really want to. Who knows, I might even end up in San Francisco."

"You'll do no such thing," Giselle said, her voice tinged with concern. "You'll go home where you belong. Don't you realize how you would hurt your mother if you did anything like that?"

"I don't think my mother cares what I do as long as I do all the housework and don't bother her."

"I happen to know differently," Giselle said. "And I think you do, too. You're just upset right now."

Francine brushed a long sweep of hair from her eye. "If I am, there's a good reason."

"Then I think you should go home and have it out with your mother and clear the air, don't you, Keith?"

"By all means." Keith's head was now thoroughly pounding. Giselle seemed more interested in Francine than she was in him. He probably bored her. Very likely she was sick to death of his hanging around every night that he possibly could.

"I'll go home if you take me," Francine said to Keith, sounding almost shy.

Giselle said, "Of course Keith will take you. We wouldn't want you out walking these streets after dark, would we, Keith?"

Now Keith was really angry. "Francine, you got here in the dark. Why can't you find your way home in the dark? It can't be that far."

"Keith!" Giselle looked appalled. "You'd never let your sister go wandering about after dark, especially after that murder. You can't let Francine do that either. I'd take her myself, except that I'm running a little late tonight."

Late. Obviously she blamed him for that. What's more, this was her way of telling him to leave. Well, all right, he could take a hint. If that was what she wanted, he'd get out and take Francine with him. And what's more, he wouldn't come back in any hurry. "Come on," he said to Francine and headed for the door.

As he stormed out and hurried down the stairs, Francine following, he almost bumped into Sammy Rupp coming out of his apartment.

7

I lay in bed, wondering why Francine had never shown up and where Keith was. Francine, I decided, had probably relented and gone home, but Keith should have been here hours ago. If Mother came home first and found him out, she'd be so mad at him. Friday nights, though, were the busiest at El Bandido, so she was always later than usual.

Although my ears were alert for the sound of her key in the lock, it was the engine of Keith's VW that I heard instead. Then nothing. Strange, I thought. I got out of bed, switched on the light, and put on my slippers and robe. Perhaps I was mistaken and it wasn't Keith's car at all but someone else's.

I went out to the living room, and as I was groping

for the light switch, I felt something—a presence. I was certain there was someone else in the room. As a chill crawled up my spine, I told myself it was probably only Grit.

I flipped on the switch and light flooded the room. Then I saw him, standing near the front door, the blue-checked shirt he had on covered with blood. I sucked in my breath, then opened my mouth to speak. Before I could get out a word, Keith whispered, "For Pete's sake, be quiet."

I paid no attention but ran to his side. "What have you done to yourself? What's happened to you?"

I saw him glance toward Mother's bedroom, so I said, "She isn't home yet, if that's what you're afraid of. I'm the only one here."

I heard his sigh of relief. "It isn't as bad as it seems," he said. "Just a small accident."

I thought he looked pale and a little sick. "You'd better come out to the kitchen and let me do something about it."

He followed me out, tossed the cardigan he was carrying onto the table, then sank into a chair. Another look at the bloody shirt in the brightness of the kitchen light, and I said, "Maybe I'd better call a doctor."

"Don't be silly. Just get a bandage and something to sterilize it. It's only a cut. I'll fix it myself."

When I returned with the medical supplies, he had removed his shirt and thrown it onto the floor. I saw

96

an ugly gash at the inner part of his arm near the elbow, and it was still oozing blood.

"If this makes you nervous, I can do it," Keith said.

"I'm okay." In the end I really surprised myself. I washed the wound, poured antiseptic into it, and wrapped it in a neat and, if I do say so, very professional-looking bandage. Then I started cleaning off the bloodstains on his face. "How did you get them there?" I asked.

He shrugged. "I guess I must have had blood on my hands and then wiped my face. I don't know." He turned his palms up to stare bewilderedly at the stains that had now dried on them.

"How about telling me what happened."

"I told you—I had an accident—with the car."

"Oh, no," I exclaimed, visualizing bodies lying all over the road.

"Don't get excited. It wasn't anything bad. There wasn't anyone else involved—no other car, I mean."

"Then how did you have an accident?"

He sighed as if he hated talking about it. "It was just one of those things. I suppose I was going a little too fast. I lost control on a curve, went into an oversteer, and hit a streetlight. I spun around in a crazy way and took it on the driver's side. The window smashed and the door jammed. I had to put pressure on the cracked glass with my fist to break enough away so that I could reach through and grab the door handle from the outside to get it open. I suppose some of the broken glass got me."

"Mother isn't going to like this a bit, not after spending all that money on the car."

"Well, just don't tell her. She'd only get all upset over nothing. The car isn't all that much damaged and neither am I. Do you think you can keep a secret for once?"

"What do you mean, for once? When have I ever said anything to give you away—anytime? And there were lots of times I could have."

"I'm sorry," he said. "I didn't mean that. It's just that I'm still shook up—and I have a rotten headache."

I got up to get the bottle of aspirin we kept in the kitchen cupboard and a glass of water. "Here, you'd better take two," I said, handing him the tablets. He swallowed the pills and drained the glass.

"How come you're calling it an accident when you're always telling me that Freud says there are no such things as accidents?" I asked.

"Freud never had a VW. If the air pressure in the front and rear tires isn't kept at the right ratio, you can get into an oversteer, which was what happened to me. Believe me, it was an accident."

I had the feeling there was more to it than that, but I didn't pursue the subject because he sounded so defensive. I thought sadly of another time long ago when he *had* confided in me. Almost every day after school in Willow Orchard, he and I would ride Mr. Walgren's horses. Mr. Walgren lived not much more than a block from us. He had what Ralph called a gentleman's farm with several horses that he let us take out because they weren't getting enough exercise. Keith taught me how to ride bareback. It was such fun. We'd go as far as Sutter's Pond, and sometimes we'd stop there awhile and have long conversations about life. I was so proud that I had a big brother who had that much time for me, and our talks made me feel so grown up. But all that closeness had disappeared out here.

I picked up the blue-checked shirt from the floor and examined it. Not only was it covered with dried blood, but the sleeve on the arm where he'd wounded himself was badly cut. I said, "Mending is never going to fix this—even if we could get out the bloodstains. I think you'd better just throw the shirt away. How about your sweater? Did you ruin that too?"

"No, I wasn't wearing it. I'd taken it off and thrown it into the backseat."

"I'll get rid of the shirt for you. If I sneak it into the trash on the day of the pickup, Mother will never notice."

"And please don't tell her. If she ever finds out, I'll have to go all through that same old business again. She'll call in the Lord Chief Justice and—"

"Don Justice?"

"Who else? He seems to have the last word on all my affairs these days."

I laughed and, for the first time that night, saw Keith

smile. It was only a little smile, but at least he no longer looked like the desperate creature I'd caught skulking into the house.

"What about the car?" I asked.

"It's not too bad. I'll take it someplace in the morning and have the glass replaced and the door fooled with. It shouldn't cost too much. I think I can swing it." He got to his feet, scooped up his sweater, and said, "I'm going to bed. I'm beat."

As he made for his bedroom, I thought about how different our lives were when Ralph was alive. The fact that he'd been dead for almost a year hardly seemed possible. Tears welled up in my eyes. How safe we had all felt then, never dreaming that our whole world would fall apart!

It had taken Mother six months to settle all the debts Ralph had piled up buying heavy equipment for pending jobs, leaving us with almost nothing. I suppose he had thought he would live forever and have plenty of time to pay everything off with the handsome profit he would make on all the work he had in progress. But it didn't happen that way. Mother had no choice but to sell the house, the one possession we had left. We had used the money to come out here and start "a new life."

I missed Ralph so much. He was the only father I had ever known. I could still remember how, when I was little, he would hoist me up onto his shoulders so that I could see a parade better. And he'd ride me around on his back, playing as hard as any kid. If I cried, he had a way of comforting me that made me go to him rather than to Mother. He always understood the importance of a broken doll or a slight from another kid. I knew there could never be another Ralph, because there could never again be that time to live over. I didn't want anyone trying to take Ralph's place any more than Keith did. All I wanted was that all of us go back to Willow Orchard, where our families and friends were and where we belonged.

The ring of the phone broke into my thoughts. I answered it and a woman's voice said, "Who is this— Bernadette?"

"Yes," I said.

"Is Francine with you?"

Eva, I realized. "No, she isn't."

"Do you know where she is?"

"No, I don't. She called me earlier, but I thought she would be home by now."

"Well, she's not. Did she say where she was going?"

"Well, no, not exactly. She did mention something about Sunset Strip—but I don't think she'd really go there." I remembered, too, that she had talked about going to Olivia Remy's tarot class, but I was sure she was just trying to worry me.

"That kid—this isn't the first time she's done something like this." Eva sounded more angry than worried.

"Well, never mind. She's probably staying with some girlfriend."

Although I doubted it, I said, "Yes, that's probably what she's doing."

When I hung up, I tried to figure out where Francine might have gone. Nothing came to mind. I was sure, though, that she hadn't gone any of the places that she'd threatened. Then where was she this late at night? As I began to worry, the thought ran through my head that I would really miss Francine when we went back to Willow Orchard.

8

On Saturday Keith had taken off early, before Louise was up, to have the window on his VW replaced, a job that was accomplished with no problems. However, fixing the dented door was going to cost more than he could spare. He decided to live with it as it was until he could better afford the repair, and tell Louise that someone must have gotten to him in the parking lot at school. He was also careful to wear long sleeves to keep the sight of his cut arm from her. He knew she would worry herself to death about the safety of his little car and about his driving.

By Sunday, although his arm was healing nicely, his psyche was doing anything but well. He was still very concerned about Giselle and their relationship, feeling a little unsure of exactly what he wanted from her. Nothing, he told himself. It wasn't a case of what she could do for him but one of what he could do for her. He could help her get over her reliance upon superstition as a way of coping with life.

She was all he could think of that day. After dinner, when the phone rang and neither Louise nor Bernadette jumped to the summons, he said, "I'll get it."

As soon as Keith heard Giselle's voice on the other end of the line, he forgot everything but the warm feeling of blood racing through his veins. "Oh, yes, Giselle," he made himself say in a voice not too anxious— a shade casual, in fact. Mustn't let her know what power she had over him. Yet the fact that she'd called him had to mean something significant.

"Keith, can you come over tonight? As soon as possible?" she asked.

Could he! Great Zot!

Keith bounded up the stairs, two at a time, passing Sammy Rupp, who was on his way down. The big guy was probably coming from Giselle's apartment, Keith thought. Normally he would have felt a pang of resentment. Tonight he was too eager to see her to waste that much emotion on Sammy. When he reached her landing, he forced himself to slow down. No need to appear too anxious.

For once she had closed her door. He gave a quick

rap, then stood playing with his car keys. In a moment, the door opened a crack and Giselle peered out cautiously. "Keith?"

"It's only me. What are you afraid of?"

"Come in." As soon as he entered, she shut the door tightly behind him. Her dark eyes lacked their usual welcome. He moved to touch her arm and ask what was the matter. Before he could get the words out, she drew abruptly away. Then she motioned toward a divan. "Sit down, Keith."

Keith picked up several magazines and placed them on top of another stack on the coffee table. He sat down, expecting her to do the same. Instead, she paced the floor. "What's the matter, Giselle?" he asked. "You act like I've come to burgle the place."

"Do I? I didn't mean to." She gave him something that was supposed to pass for a smile, but he could tell her mind was elsewhere. Everything about her seemed different today. Instead of wearing one of her usual costumes, she wore a simple dark green pullover and matching skirt. This was the first time he had seen her in anything conventional. She looked like a high school kid, he thought. "What's up?"

"Why, nothing. Does something have to be up just because I ask you to come over?"

"I don't know," Keith said.

"I just thought we could visit."

"Fine with me." He waited for her to initiate some

conversation. When she didn't, he said, "How was your party the other night?"

He thought that she looked at him sharply. "You mean Friday night? The night you and Francine were here?"

"Yes."

"It was okay." Her eyes seemed to avoid his as she said, "How'd you make out with Francine? Did she give you any trouble?"

He had no desire to talk about Francine. He wanted to talk about Giselle and his relationship with her. "There are more interesting subjects than Francine," he said.

She studied him for a moment, as if trying to decide how to broach whatever it was that was bothering her. Finally, she said, "Keith, I want you to tell me something."

"Anything," he offered generously.

"This is serious, Keith. Very serious. I'm going to ask you something, and I want you to tell me the truth. Now, whatever you tell me, I'll believe. And please don't think that I'll judge you. I won't. Honestly, I won't."

What the devil . . . ? "Well, ask away," he said, a little impatiently but at the same time trying to catch her serious mood.

Giselle stopped pacing and faced him. "Keith, what happened after you left here Friday night?"

So that was it. He had no intention of telling her how,

after he'd dropped off Francine, he'd circled back to her place, seen her driving away, and followed, hoping to catch up and have things out. The stupid accident had brought him to his senses. "Nothing happened. I went home."

"Then look me in the eye and tell me."

"What is this, Giselle? The third degree?"

"What did you do with Francine?"

Keith frowned. "What did you think I'd do with her? Take her out on a date?"

"No, I didn't think that at all."

Keith found himself growing angry. "Then what *did* you think? That I'd take her someplace and try to seduce her?"

"Oh, Keith," Giselle gasped, "not you."

The expression on her face frightened him. For the first time he noticed how pale she looked. "Look, Giselle, you're grilling me and I don't know what—"

"Keith, where did you take Francine when you left here?"

"I took her home."

"Keith, tell me."

"I did tell you."

"You're being evasive."

"I'm not being evasive."

"Keith, you've got to tell me what happened with Francine."

"All right," he said soberly. "Can I help it if she's

107

such a crazy kid? I set out to take her home, only with her directions, we wound up on the Strand." Keith shook his head. "I don't even want to talk about it, but I'll tell you this—Francine needs some sense knocked into her."

Giselle moaned. "How can you say that?"

"It's true," he insisted.

"She's dead and you don't even care."

"Dead . . ." Keith echoed in a small voice. That was the last thing he'd expected. "I never thought—"

"Some kids found her body this morning. They were out riding horses. She had been brutally attacked."

Stunned, he asked, "How did you find out?"

"Steve, Francine's stepfather, called me a little while ago." She shook her head sadly. "Poor Eva. What a terrible thing to happen—Francine was her only child."

"When did it happen?"

"Friday night. Sometime between eight and midnight, they think."

Keith was having a hard time taking in her words. Friday, she'd said. The same night he had given Francine a ride home. Only instead of going home, she must have gone looking for trouble. Although he had never liked Francine, now he felt guilty. Perhaps if he'd waited around for a few minutes, he could have stopped her from doing anything foolish. "Do they know who did it?"

"I don't think so. They found her out on the Peninsula someplace—I'm not sure where." Giselle sat

108

slumped on a tattered plastic hassock. "Were you—did you have anything to do with it, Keith?" she asked, her voice hesitating on the words.

Keith stiffened. "Why would you think that?"

"I don't think anything. I just want to know. Sometimes it seems as though you have such a lot of anger in you."

Anger? How could she say that? He had never been anything but gentle and kind with her. "I'll admit I was angry that night about taking Francine home, but does that have to mean I murdered her?"

"Not if you tell me you didn't."

"Tell you? Why do I have to tell you? Don't you know? Don't the tarot cards tell you everything?"

"Keith, just tell me you didn't have anything to do with Francine's death. That's all I want to hear," Giselle said.

"All right. I didn't have anything to do with Francine's death. Now, I said it. What does that prove?"

Giselle ignored the question. "Then you must go to the police. You were the last person to see her alive."

"Except the murderer—as they say in books." Keith's voice was sharp, and he could feel a muscle working along his jawline.

"You know what I mean, Keith. You might be able to help them."

"Look, Giselle, it wasn't my idea—driving Francine home. I didn't want to—remember? There's nothing I can say that will help the police. I don't know anything about her. I let her out in front of her house and went on my way. I thought she went inside. I can't help it if she didn't."

"Keith, if you don't go, I'll have to go—"

Keith shot to his feet. In an anguished voice he said, "Why are you doing this to me, Giselle? You know what could happen! What if they tried to pin her death on me? Do you want to see me executed or put away for life? Is that what you want?"

Giselle gave a bewildered shake of her head and opened her mouth to speak, but Keith raged on, "You don't believe me, do you! Maybe you'd like to see me put away—then I couldn't bother you anymore. Well, you don't have to worry. I won't bother you again." With a few long strides Keith reached the door, opened it, intending to fling himself through, then thought better of it. He turned back to find Giselle still sitting on the hassock, an anxious expression on her face.

The anger suddenly drained from him. "I thought you asked me here tonight to talk about us. That's really funny, isn't it?" He could feel his jaw muscle working like a throbbing nerve now. "You go ahead and do what you think best, Giselle."

He started to let himself out. At the same time, he heard her murmur, "Oh, Keith . . . Keith . . ."

As he closed it, the door made a hollow sound. What a fool he was. He swore he'd never try to get that close to anyone again.

9

Over a week had passed since Francine's funeral. I still couldn't believe she was dead. At odd moments of the day I'd think, *I guess I should call Francine*. Then the memory of the spicy scent of carnations would flood my senses and I would be back in the funeral parlor, staring at her closed coffin. I kept trying to block from my imagination the horror of her last moments. Murder is something that happens to people you read about in the newspapers, not to someone you know.

The papers also carried articles about the first murder. That girl, it seemed, had lived in Cerritos Beach too. Her mother was dead, and the stories made it sound as if her father had neglected her. He had no idea where she had been going that night or what she was doing out on the Peninsula. The police seemed to feel the same person had committed both crimes, because both girls had had their throats slashed. Just the thought made me shudder, imagining blood all over the place.

The papers also said that the police had no real leads to the killer. If there had been any tread marks from his car, the local horseback riders had erased them. All the police were sure of was that he was driving a small vehicle.

After the first shock, a frozen numb feeling settled over me. That was how I'd felt when the police had questioned me about Francine and her friends and her habits. I just knew that none of it was real. I was watching and hearing myself in a dream. I kept reliving that awful night, and telling myself that it was my fault she was dead. If I had met her when she had asked me to, she would probably still be alive.

When I let myself into the house after school that day, I heard Mother call from the kitchen, "Is that you, honey?"

"Yes, it's me."

She came out of the kitchen with a teacup in her hand. "I've just come home from shopping." She took her cup into the living room and sat down. "I found a blouse to go with your gray skirt."

"Oh, good," I said.

"It's on the dining table. See if you like it."

There were two bags on the dining table, one on top

of the other. I picked up the top bag and peeked inside. "This it?" I pulled out a white blouse daintily trimmed with lace. "It's sweet." I draped it in front of me and walked over for Mother's approval. "How does it look?"

She eyed it appraisingly. "Nice. It was an awfully good buy—on sale for half price." She sipped her tea. "Why don't you try it on?"

I knew that this was her way of trying to cheer me up because I'd felt so low about what had happened to Francine. "Okay." I nodded toward the other package on the dining table. "What's in that?"

"Just a shirt I bought for Keith. He seems to be running short. Of course, if he's going to start lending shirts to other people, it's no wonder."

I perked up my ears. "Lending shirts?"

"Oh, he lent his blue-checked shirt to some friend. Can you imagine? Gave it to him, probably."

So that was what he had told Mother. And I wasn't about to tell her anything different. Fortunately I had disposed of the shirt in the trash, which had already been picked up, so there was no chance of her finding out.

I left Mother finishing her tea and headed for my bedroom. There was no point in telling her about the accident. Keith was hard enough to live with these days. He seemed irritable and depressed. If he had to make explanations about what had happened, no one would be able to stand him.

The thought of Keith's shirt brought back the memory of that terrible, terrible night. Francine's call. Keith. Everything. And that same night, Francine lying someplace, bleeding to death, a murderer leaning over her . . . Blood. *Both girls had their throats slashed.* All that ran through my head was the sight of Keith that night with blood all over his shirt and even on his face.

After school the following day I headed directly for The Mandrake Root, hoping to catch Giselle alone and talk to her. I could think of no other way to find out about Keith. If he had visited her that Friday night, as Francine had insisted when she'd called, and if he'd stayed there all evening, then there was nothing to worry about.

Keith could never kill anyone anyhow, I kept telling myself. And yet my mind kept magnifying his behavior until I wasn't sure what I thought. Why was he always reading books on abnormal psychology? And whether he knew it or not, he was very possessive of Mother. Look how he'd blown up at the idea of Don's marrying her. He had not been at all like that before Ralph's death. And how often he grew mad at something or someone—even Francine. Something else came back to me: the other girl—the hitchhiker. What was it he had said? Something about hitchhikers getting what they asked for. My head swam with unanswered questions.

As I neared the shop, a man I recognized as the police detective who had questioned me earlier came out.

Quickly, I ducked into the entry of a nearby antiques store, where I pretended to window-shop. I just couldn't bear facing him, for fear he'd be able to see into my head. I waited until he drove off, then approached the shop cautiously and peered through the window to satisfy myself that there were no police inside before I entered.

Inside, Giselle stood behind the counter, talking to Steve Rinko, Francine's stepfather. Although he never glanced my way, his voice lowered when I walked in. I pretended to browse through an expensive edition of the Cabala while my ears strained to listen.

"Eva will not be herself again until they catch this bloodthirsty devil." His voice sounded grim.

"Lieutenant Dyer says they figure it's some psycho," Giselle said.

"Pah!" Steve sneered. "What do cops know about such things? Now they hire head doctors to tell them their business. Psycho! All killers are psychos. So what does that tell them? Nothing. My psychics could tell them more."

After my recent thoughts about Keith, I could feel my stomach tighten.

"What does Madame Kasha say?" Giselle asked.

"Madame is too old to go any higher than the astral plane anymore. Where does it happen? she asks. Out at the bend, up in the hills near the old stables, I tell her. Aha, she says, and who lives in those hills? Olivia

Remy, the witch! What are you listening to? I ask her. Murderers? Atheists? Suicides? They do not know any more than you. Five of my best psychics say different. Closer to home, they say, closer to the shop, someone who comes in here, or hangs around here. And it makes sense. Who did Francine know? People close to the shop, not someone from Olivia's place."

The book slid from my hands and fell with a thump to the floor. Hastily I retrieved it. Then I looked over to Steve, feeling like a trapped animal. "I'm sorry. But it didn't get hurt."

Now he recognized me. "Oh, hello, Bernadette," he said, and fixed me with an even stare that made me feel terribly uneasy. Steve gave classes in ESP. Perhaps he could read minds. To my relief he turned back to Giselle. "You hold the fort. I'm going to get on home." Although a stocky man, he moved quickly to the door with purposeful strides. "You can lock up when you leave," he called back.

After he left, Giselle turned to me. "Can I do anything for you, Bernadette?"

"I'm just browsing." I put the Cabala back on the shelf, picked up another book, and thumbed through it. "He was talking about Francine, wasn't he?"

She gave a weary sigh. "Yes."

Usually she sparkled. Today I thought she looked dull. "Why do they think it was someone Francine knew?"

"*They* don't think anything yet. It's Eva who keeps saying Francine would never accept a ride with a stranger.

I think Eva knows better, but now that Francine is dead, she feels it would be unkind to her memory to say so. But of course, with all those psychics saying—"

"Do you think they're right?"

"I don't know what to think. They're awfully good." For a moment she stared off into space, her eyes clouded. Then she roused and turned back to me with a smile. "Well, enough of gloomy thoughts. How are you?"

"Oh, fine."

"And how is that big brother of yours?"

"Keith's okay."

I pretended to look through the book, but I watched her out of the corner of my eye. "It's sure a good thing Keith was with you that night, or I expect they'd even be questioning him."

Giselle shot me a startled glance, then dropped her eyes and began fiddling with a candle display. She said nothing.

"I said, it's a good thing Keith—"

"I heard what you said."

I waited but nothing came. "Well, he *was* with you, wasn't he?"

When she looked up again, her eyes held a guarded expression. "Did Keith tell you that?"

I didn't want to mention Francine's phone call, so I said, "Yes."

"I suppose he told you that he was here until quite late that night—eleven or twelve."

"Oh, yes," I said, happy that she was confirming what

117

I wanted to hear. "Well, I guess it's pretty silly to talk about Keith. What would he have to do with anything like that, anyhow?"

Giselle was quiet for a moment. Then she said, "If you don't want anything, Bernadette, I have to get busy and open some new stock." In another moment she had disappeared into the back room.

Well, there was no point in staying around any longer. Keith had been at Giselle's all Friday night. That was all I'd wanted to know. As I stood mulling over the fact, the phone rang. Giselle answered in the back room. I picked up my book bag and started to leave.

"A week ago last Friday night?" I heard Giselle say.

I stopped in my tracks and listened.

"The Kleins' party? Oh, yes. Yes, you have the right person. I did the readings that night. Yes, I think I remember. You're the one with the two Siamese cats. You say Ming really did have only two kittens? Well, I was right then, wasn't I? The sixteenth? Yes, I'll be free. I'll be glad to do your party."

I felt sick. Keith could not have stayed until eleven or twelve o'clock if she'd read at a party that Friday night. Why had she lied? Would she try to protect him if she thought he'd murdered someone? I shivered, hugged my book bag to my chest, and fled from the shop.

I hurried up the street, my mind a jumble of scary thoughts. The day was overcast. Wisps of fog started to drift in off the ocean, which was only a few blocks away. I felt chilled and pulled my sweater closer about me. As I put distance between myself and the shop, I became aware of the quick tread of soft-soled shoes behind me. Startled, I turned to glimpse Mark Keeper dogging my footsteps. I hadn't seen him since that night at my house, and I'd hoped to never see him again, so I began to walk faster. When his steps quickened too, I knew he was following me. Angry, I spun around. "What do you want?"

Beside me now, he said, "I just want to talk to you. It's important."

I studied him. He looked pale and anxious. Red lids gave his eyes the look of someone who either slept little or cried a lot. I almost felt sorry for him. "Well, if you just want to talk—"

"That's all I want—I just want to talk to you." Then he looked at a loss.

I was getting impatient. "Well, what do you want to talk about?"

He hesitated for a moment, then said, "Well, I've been thinking—about what you said—you know, about my being hexed and all."

"I didn't really mean you were. It was just an idea."

"Yeah, but I think I am. At least—I guess I should find out about it."

In spite of my qualms about him, I was beginning to grow fascinated. Perhaps he *was* hexed. He certainly

119

looked it. "Do you have any idea who could have done it?"

He shook his head. "I thought maybe I did—for a while. Now I just don't know anymore."

"It would have to be a witch. Only a witch would know how to do it."

Mark stopped abruptly. "You're right! You know, I never thought of that. Sure! That was what was wrong all the time—it has to be a witch."

I suspected he didn't know quite as much about these things as I did. Feeling superior, I said, "Well, of course. Sammy would tell you I'm right."

"That's what I wanted to ask you. That guy Sammy—you know where he lives?"

"Yes, on B Street. In the same building Giselle Fox lives in. I don't know the number, though. I went there once with—with a friend." I remembered Francine looking into Sammy's two-hundred-dollar crystal ball and saying, "All I can see is myself." Poor Francine. I said, "Sammy likes company. You could go see him."

"Could you show me where the building is?"

I hesitated. "Well, I—"

"Please. I just gotta find out what to do."

I decided that he very likely *was* hexed. If anyone could help him, Sammy could. "Okay," I said. "I'll take you to Sammy's. It's only a few minutes' walk."

Along the way he made no conversation, but in front of Sammy's apartment house, he said, "What if he's not home?"

"If he's not home, his mother will tell you when he'll be back."

"Come with me. You can explain better than I can."

I shrugged. "Okay. But I can't stay very long."

Sammy's mother, a skinny, shriveled-up woman who looked too old to be anyone's mother, answered the door. Her black-raisin eyes glared at both of us.

"May we see Sammy, Mrs. Rupp?" I asked.

"What you want with Sammy?"

"We'd just like to see him."

"You come for a cure? Sammy can cure a body most as good as his pa, but you gotta pay."

"We don't want a cure, Mrs. Rupp. We just want to see Sammy. Can we come in?"

She grunted but didn't move out of our way. From someplace in the apartment, Sammy's voice boomed, "Who is it, Ma?"

"Some young'uns here about a cure," she barked back to him.

"Tell 'em to come in. I'll be right out."

She let us into a small, drab living room that smelled of sauerkraut and sausage. "Sammy's a powwower like his pa but not near so good yet," she said.

"I'm not gonna be no powwower, Ma. I'm gonna be a healer. That's what you call 'em now." Sammy came striding out of the kitchen with a piece of pie in his fist. "Hey, Bernadette," he exclaimed at the sight of me, "you come to see me. How about a piece of shoofly pie?"

121

"No thanks, Sammy," I said, anxious to be gone. "It's Mark who wants to see you. Maybe you know him from the shop."

Whether he did or not, he said, "Oh, sure. Never did know what was your name, though." He wolfed down some of the pie. As his mother watched, he nodded approval. "Good, Ma." Then he said, "Why don't you go redd up the table, Ma?"

Mrs. Rupp gave both of us a sour look. "Just like his pa," she grumbled. "Never a cent for all his powwowin'." She hobbled off and disappeared into the kitchen.

"Just got through on the job," Sammy said, finishing off the pie. He still wore work clothes, blue jeans and a T-shirt that barely covered his big belly. "Ma's always at me to charge for healin' folks. Can't understand I'd lose all my power doin' somethin' like that."

"We don't want any powwowing, Sammy." I glanced uneasily toward the kitchen, thinking that Mark probably wouldn't want any more people than necessary in on his problem. "Could we go to your room and talk?"

"Why, sure." Sammy wiped a sticky hand on his T-shirt as he led the way.

Sammy's room held a cot for a bed, a crude table for a desk, an unpainted bookcase, and a few kitchen chairs. Cracked blue linoleum, its design long faded, covered the floor. The room would have had a monasterylike austerity except for the colorful zodiac posters brightening the walls and the crystal ball sitting on a piece of black velvet on the table.

For the most part Sammy's bookcase held books on divination. I noticed *The Long-Lost Friend* sandwiched between the *I Ching* and *The Seventh Book of Moses*, and I thought of Francine. She had pulled the book out to look at on our visit. Immediately Sammy had warned her to be careful. "It was my pa's," he'd said. "Back in Pennsylvany where I come from, that there book's the powwower's bible, you know." Francine had shrugged and made a saucy remark. Poor, poor Francine.

I tore my thoughts from her as Sammy said, "Well, take a chair. Sit down."

Sammy sat on the edge of the cot while Mark and I perched stiffly on the kitchen chairs. Immediately, Sammy went off on a long story about holding the apartment manager's scarab ring in his hand. "I tell you, the minute I touched that there ring, I knowed I once was livin' in Egypt. I knowed I once was somebody." Then his eyes grew sad. "Don't know what I done though— musta really done somethin' bad to wind up like I done in this life. I figger now it's my job to study and learn and get to be a big healer. Then I won't botch up in my next incarnation."

Sammy would go on and on, I knew, so I said, "Sammy, I can't stay very long. Mark wants to ask you for some help."

"Oh, sure," Sammy said, and stared at Mark questioningly.

Mark glanced at me. "You tell him."

I said, "Mark thinks he's been hexed."

123

Sammy's round, cherubic face went instantly somber. "You sure?"

Mark nodded. "I think so."

"You sufferin' from the melancholy?"

"Yeah—I guess."

"You feel all put out and put down?"

Again Mark nodded.

"Can't do no work?"

"Yeah—I mean, no, I can't."

Sammy shook his head sympathetically. "I know how you feel, boy. I was feelin' so grieved, and no matter what I done, it never got no better."

"Yeah . . ." Mark murmured.

"Now I ain't sayin' yes and I ain't sayin' no, but it sounds like maybe somebody got to you. When it happened to me, all I knowed was I was in one terrible predicament. Why, I was so bad off, I couldn't do my work, couldn't do nothin'—and I was gettin' that far, I didn't care no more."

Mark watched him anxiously.

Sammy sighed. "Never could find out who behexed me, either. If'n it was now, I'd be able to know—got the power now." He tapped his head. "If'n it wasn't for this here steel plate in my head, he'da got me for sure, though. That's how a witch works. He's gotta send the hexin' vibrations into your head. With this here plate now, nobody can get through no more."

"Mark can't get a steel plate put in his head, Sammy," I said.

124

"No, don't suppose he could."

Mark appealed to Sammy. "Must be something I can do."

"First, we gotta find out who behexed you."

"Then what?"

"Then we do somethin' about it."

"What?"

"Now don't hurry me, boy. I gotta look it up." Sammy got off the cot and went to his closet. "Got a book of my pa's hid away here somewheres. Oughta tell us somethin'."

Sammy opened the door and I had to blink twice to believe my eyes. A foldout of a *Playboy* nude, cuddling a Siamese kitten, hung inside. That was the last thing I expected Sammy to have. Embarrassed, I glanced over to see if Mark had noticed. Fortunately, he sat—elbow cupped in one hand, chin cupped in the other—staring off, I guess, into the dark world of the bewitched.

Sammy rummaged around the floor behind stacks of old magazines until he drew out a small black book that looked like a journal. "Found it," he said, getting to his feet. As he started to close the door, the nude caught his eye. He stared for a long moment, then turned away and said with a sigh, "Sure do love cats. Wish the owner of this place wasn't so all-fired down on keepin' pets."

Would a grown man hang a picture of a nude only because it had a cat on it? I asked myself. Probably no one but Sammy.

He drew a chair up to the table, licked a finger, and

started to slowly thumb through the black book. Finally he found what he was looking for. "Just the way I thought. Knowed I was right, oney I didn't wanna take a chance on tellin' you wrong. Says here you gotta cut off a lock of the witch's hair and bury it eight feet deep. It was that eight feet part I disremembered."

"How am I going to do that?" Mark asked.

"Easy. You get him asleep. No trouble that way."

"Okay. But how do I know who the witch is?"

"Well, now, might take a little time, but most probably I can find out—if Michael's of a mind to tell me."

"Michael's one of the archangels who communicates with Sammy," I explained to Mark. Then I said to Sammy, "The only person I know of that you could call a witch is that Olivia."

Sammy said, "There's plenty more witches 'round 'sides that woman. There's white witches and black witches. No harm in bein' a witch. It's all in how you use your powers. Giselle upstairs now, she oney tries to do good."

"Is she a witch?" I asked.

"Well, sure. Giselle has lotsa power, lotsa ESP, too. That's all it takes. I keep tellin' you, Bernadette, you can be the same way." He grabbed my hand and turned it palm up. "Look at that. Look at all them X's. You was born with 'em. Lotsa ESP—you just gotta learn how to use it."

Mark got up to look at my palm, too. "He's right. You got a lot of X's."

126

As I drew my hand away, I checked my wristwatch to find it was getting late. "I've got to go," I said, grabbing my book bag. "I'm sorry, Sammy, but I'll be late for dinner. Mark can stay, though." When Sammy moved to follow me, I added, "That's all right. I'll let myself out."

I dashed off before either Sammy or Mark could slow me down with conversation; and to my great relief, as I made my way through the living room and out the front door, I saw no sign of Mrs. Rupp.

10

After Louise left for work that night, Keith sprawled on the living room divan, his long legs stretched out to rest on the woven top of the only stool in the room. He glowered at the psychology book on his lap in an attempt to force concentration, but his mind wandered. Oh, well, he knew the stuff anyhow, knew it as well as the instructor.

Probably he should have gone to work instead of sitting around, boning up for an exam he could pass with his eyes closed. Besides, who could think anyhow with the racket Bernadette was making out in the kitchen as she did the dishes?

For days now, Keith had had the feeling that the bottom had fallen out of everything, and all because of

128

Francine. Why had she had to turn up that Friday night? Why had she had to get herself killed? Why had her death had to come between him and Giselle? He had the strange feeling that Francine's death and what it had done to his relationship with Giselle was some kind of punishment for old crimes. He knew he was being irrational, yet he couldn't stop himself from feeling that way.

His mind kept returning to Giselle. If she had cared about him at all, she would never have accused him like that. When you really cared about people, you believed the best of them. You knew what they were like inside, and that was all that counted. He could never have turned against *her*. All of which proved just what she thought of him.

To hell with it. Who needed her? She was years older than he was anyhow. In four years she would be thirty and probably a hag. Besides, who needed two little kids? He could just see them hopping all over his lap, begging for piggyback rides. Sticky-fingered moppets. What would they call him? Keith? Uncle Keith? *Uncle Keith, buy me an ice-cream cone. Uncle Keith, fix my bicycle.* Who needed that? Two little brown-haired kids with big dark eyes. . . soft pink lips . . . warm little bodies . . . dimples—Giselle's dimples . . . To hell with it.

Keith called to Bernadette in the kitchen, "Could you make a little less noise with those dishes?"

Sudden silence. Even the sound of running water stopped. Then he could hear her moving around on what sounded like tiptoe. Then a slow metallic grinding. The can opener, of course. A clinking of something against tin. A spoon against a can? Sure. She was feeding Grit. Now her pussyfooting quiet was even worse than all the noise she'd been making. "You don't have to be that quiet," he shouted.

Bernadette came out of the kitchen and into the dining area. "I'm sorry. I forgot you were studying. I'm through now, so I won't make any more noise."

Keith couldn't help glancing at her suspiciously. She was acting just too polite. At any other time she would have made a big to-do over other people's rights. "I didn't mean you had to go around in your stocking feet and act like someone was sick."

For an instant there was a flash of something in her eyes that puzzled him. Then it disappeared. She said, "Is it okay if I get a book and read out here?"

He shrugged. "Go ahead."

"I won't bother you."

"Okay, okay," he said shortly.

When she returned, Bernadette settled in a chair across from him. Without a word, she opened her book and buried her nose in it. As time went by, Keith realized she was only pretending to read. Every time he looked up, he caught her staring at him. He began to feel uncomfortable.

Finally she said, "Remember Pebble Creek Park, Keith?"

Keith looked up from his book. "Sure."

"Remember the time I fell into the creek with all my clothes on and you pulled me out?"

Keith smiled in spite of himself. "I remember you went running to Dad crying you were drownded. And for the next week you told everyone you met that you'd drownded in Pebble Creek Park. What made you think of that place?"

"Oh, the book I'm reading. The people are out on a picnic. That made me think of it. I sure miss that park, don't you?"

"I don't know. I haven't really thought about it."

"Remember Leslie Horvath?"

"The redhead who looked like she didn't have any eyelashes?"

"Oh, she had eyelashes, Keith—beautiful eyelashes—and long. They were just golden, that's all. Most likely she uses mascara now. I'm sure if you saw her now, you'd think she had beautiful eyelashes. She sure was crazy about you."

Keith made a face.

"She was, Keith. Remember when she was in high school how she'd come home every day and bake cookies and bring them over? That was to impress you."

"I remember her making cookies once—not every day."

131

"Oh, it was more than that. I know it was. I'll bet Leslie is really gorgeous now."

"Leslie!"

"Well, with that beautiful red hair—and she really was pretty, you've got to admit that."

"I never noticed."

"And she really was crazy about you. She really was."

Keith thought, Now what is she up to? "All I remember about Leslie is that she was always either very high or very low. Definitely manic-depressive."

"You're exaggerating, Keith." She smiled tolerantly. "Anyhow, I sure miss Willow Orchard, don't you?"

"Not much."

"Oh, Keith, you've got to admit it's a pretty town."

"It's okay, I guess."

"It has all those lovely big trees on all the streets. In the summer they make everything so nice and shady, and in the fall they turn such pretty colors. All we have out here are skinny old palm trees that grow so high you almost can't find them."

Keith shrugged.

"You know, I got another letter from Gran yesterday."

"Gran Crenshaw?"

She nodded. "She says she wishes we had never moved so far away. She misses us, Keith. I miss her, too, don't you?"

"A little, maybe. Of all of them back there, she was

132

the nicest to me even though I wasn't really family. I never knew either of my own grandmothers, so I really appreciated her."

Bernadette sighed. "Do you think Mother will ever get married again?"

Keith frowned. "What's that got to do with Willow Orchard and Pebble Creek Park and Leslie Horvath?"

"Oh—nothing, I guess. It's just that I was thinking about how much better everything was. I mean, we were happy when we lived back there."

"It wasn't all *that* great."

"Well, you've got to admit we were happy there."

"Once, maybe."

Bernadette looked thoughtful for a moment. "Keith, did it ever bother you—not having a mother like other kids? I mean, before Ralph married Mother?"

The question surprised him. All of a sudden she sounded so mature. "I guess it bothered me some." If anything had bothered him, it was the fact that his mother had died from a ruptured appendix only three weeks after bearing him. He often wondered if his birth had contributed to the ailment. Yet whenever the thought occurred to him, he pushed it away. Of course he wasn't responsible for her death. What did a ruptured appendix have to do with pregnancy, anyhow? Nothing. But why did he think about death so often—about hers, about his dad's? Always it left him feeling bereft and betrayed. Everyone who loves me leaves me.

Bernadette broke into his thoughts. "How did it bother you?"

He had lost the thread of their conversation. "How did what bother me?"

"Not having a mother. I mean, did it make you feel like you'd been born without an arm or a leg—like you were odd or different from everybody else?"

Keith was astonished. She had put her finger on the feeling that had plagued him throughout childhood, a feeling that he could never quite analyze, much less verbalize. "How could you know how it felt?"

"I guess because I never had a father."

"But that was only when you were a baby. How can you remember that far back?"

"I don't know, but I do."

"I can't believe it."

Bernadette gave her head an adamant shake. "You never forget something like that."

"But you had Dad. He was a good father to you."

"Oh, I know. He was wonderful. And I miss him. It means a lot, having a father like Ralph in a family. It makes everything—well, kind of safe."

"I know," Keith said. Since his father's death he'd had the feeling that the whole world was falling apart. He could almost understand Bernadette's love affair with Willow Orchard. Somehow she couldn't understand that going back there just couldn't bring back the life they'd once known. If anything, it could only make all of them feel the loss more.

134

"That's why I don't want Mother to marry someone like Don. I mean, he's not my idea of a father."

"Nor mine," Keith said.

Bernadette turned an intense gaze on him. "I sometimes have the strongest feeling that my own father is still alive."

"Your father!" he exclaimed incredulously. "Oh, Bunny," he said, using a long-forgotten pet name, "you mustn't try to convince yourself of anything like that. You'd only be fooling yourself."

"Oh, I don't mean that I really believe it. I know it isn't true, but it's something I like to imagine. I always place him in the most wonderful places, like in an old Victorian house in San Francisco or in a villa in Italy. He's always very intelligent and we have the best talks. He answers all my hard questions. What I mean is that, in my imagination, he seems very much alive."

"That's fantasy."

"What's wrong with that?"

"Nothing. Just as long as you know that's all it is."

"Of course I know. But that doesn't keep me from imagining. I even imagine us back in Willow Orchard." She looked thoughtful for a moment. "Just out of curiosity, of all the men we knew back there, who would you say would make a good husband for Mother?"

"How would I know?" he said, amused. "Don't you think we should let Louise decide that?"

She ignored the question. "What do you think of Mr. Naimon?"

"Matt Naimon, the undertaker?"

"Yes. After all, he's never been married."

"You're darned right. He's a confirmed bachelor. At his age, he's still living with his mother. I suspect he's never resolved his Oedipal conflicts." Keith shook his head. "I can't believe you're that desperate to go back to Willow Orchard."

"I really think we should go back, Keith. If you tried, I believe you could talk Mother into it. After all, you don't want her to marry Don, and if we're out here just for the colleges, well, there are plenty of colleges close enough for you to go to. We'd be safe there. You'd . . ." Her voice trailed away.

There was something about the way she said *safe* that bothered him. "What do you mean by safe—in what way?"

She dropped her eyes. "Oh, you know. I mean, we wouldn't have to worry about getting robbed or anything like that."

Somehow he couldn't quite believe that she felt that insecure. "You're sounding very paranoid. Are you sure there isn't something else on your mind?"

"Oh, no," she said quickly.

He leaned forward and looked deeply into her eyes. "Look, Bunny, I think I know how you feel, but there just isn't anything I can do about it. We can't just pick up and leave now. It's not practical. We wouldn't have the money, anyhow. Eventually you'll get used to it out here. Honestly you will."

He could tell that she didn't believe him. Feeling impotent, he closed his book and got up. "I'm going out," he said. He went back to his room and picked up a sweater before heading for the front door. Although he could feel her eyes boring into the back of his neck, he never glanced at her. "Be back later," he said, and hurried out the door, wishing that he was already earning the kind of money that could change their lives.

He drove around aimlessly for a time, then made his way past Giselle's apartment, surprised to find her windows dark. Feeling dejected, he drove slowly home. When he reached his own driveway, he noticed a sedan parked in front of his house. A stocky man in a gray suit got out and met Keith at the front porch. "You Keith McKay?" he asked, his tone sober.

Although the man was in plain clothes, Keith guessed instantly that he was a policeman.

11

Every few minutes I got up and looked out the living room window. "Does Don have to pay something—I mean, put up bail money or something to get Keith out of jail?" I asked my mother.

"I wish you'd relax, Bernadette. You're making me nervous. Staring out the window every few seconds won't bring them here any faster." Mother sat quietly, but her fingers drummed on the divan's armrest. "Of course he doesn't have to put up bail. Keith isn't arrested. It's all a big mistake."

Oh, I hope so, I thought. And if it's not a mistake, please, God, make them believe it is. My stomach felt all tight inside. I tried to keep from thinking, because my thoughts only made me hate myself for not feeling certain about Keith's innocence. Sure, there were times when I got mad at Keith, but I really *did* love him. I told myself now that if he *had* murdered anyone, there was a good reason. He was sick. Or he was possessed by some evil soul who wandered the astral plane. Neither of which he could help, or be blamed for.

As I stared out the window, my thoughts were interrupted by the sight of the big shiny blue Buick I recognized as Don's. "Here they come," I cried, and raced to the front door to fling it open and wait anxiously as Keith strode up the walk. When he reached me, I threw my arms around him and began to cry.

Keith patted my shoulder. "Don't cry." Then he freed himself from my tight grip and drew me with him into the house. "It's all right."

Mother hurried over and gave him a half-strained, half-affectionate hug. "Now you mustn't let it upset you, Keith. It's all over—all a big mistake." Then she turned to me and put an arm around me. "Don't cry, honey. There's nothing to cry about. Keith's home—it's all a mistake."

"What's all this?" Don's voice boomed as he came through the door, swinging it shut behind him. He made a sympathetic noise when he saw my tears. "Aw, now, there's nothing to cry about. Keith's home and everything's fine. There was no reason to hold him."

Mother said, "Why don't I get us all some coffee? I've been keeping it hot."

"Good idea," Don said. As Mother disappeared into the kitchen, he gingerly settled his large frame on our spindly divan.

Keith handed me a rumpled handkerchief. "Here, dry your eyes." Then he sat down in a chair across from Don.

I knew my tears were making Keith uncomfortable, so I stabbed at my eyes with his somewhat soiled handkerchief. Then I visualized him using the same handkerchief to wipe sweat from his brow under the burning heat of third-degree lamps, and my eyes filled up again.

In another moment Mother came back, carrying a tray of steaming cups. She served Don and Keith, then handed a cup to me. "Here, I fixed one for you, too. It will make you feel better. And for goodness' sake sit down with it. You'll make everyone nervous just standing there like that."

I took the cup and perched on a chair near Keith.

"What happened, Keith?" Mother asked. "Was it very bad?"

"Not as bad as it probably would have been if Don hadn't shown. Mostly it was just a lot of waiting around until they checked up."

Although I'd said nothing about it, I couldn't help resenting the fact that Mother had appealed to Don for help.

Don said, "I know Lieutenant Dyer personally. He's going to marry one of the waitresses on the day shift. That helped speed things up, I think."

"Thank goodness for that," Mother said.

"The thing is," Don continued, "that night someone saw Keith with Francine, saw them getting into his car." Don turned to Keith with a frown. "Keith, you should have come forward and told them you gave her a ride home that night. Might have helped them get a line on the real killer."

"Why didn't you, Keith?" Mother asked.

Keith sounded sulky as he said, "Oh, I don't know— I didn't know anything anyhow. Then too, I just couldn't see much point in getting all of you involved."

Oh, sure, I said to myself. I knew darned well who he didn't want to get involved—Giselle.

"Where did you meet Francine that night?" Mother asked.

Keith's glance shifted to his feet. "Oh, I was down in The Village."

Don put in, "Dyer said something about some apartment house."

"Yes—well, I was visiting someone. Francine just happened to show up at the same place and I drove her home. That's all."

Mother said, "Who were you visiting, Keith?"

"No one you know."

I spoke up. "He was visiting Giselle Fox, that's who." It was time Mother knew about Keith's carrying on with an older woman.

Keith fixed me with an angry stare, furious, I supposed, because I was telling on him. I didn't care, though. I didn't regret my words one bit.

"Giselle Fox," Mother mused. "Isn't that the girl who works for Eva?"

I said, "Yes. And she's divorced and has two kids."

The worried expression in Mother's eyes made Keith look squirmy. Then he grew defensive. "Look, stop making a case out of it. She's a friend—at least, she was—that's all. You don't have to get so uptight. I don't see her anymore anyhow."

Don relieved the tension by changing the subject. "Well, anyhow, all's well that ends well. They didn't even book Keith. Had nothing to go on. They *did* check out a bloodstain in his car, but it wasn't Francine's blood type. It was his. The main thing was Keith's not coming forward from the start. Well, I guess he's learned his lesson now." He looked at Keith as if expecting agreement. Instead, Keith just glowered down at his long legs.

Don set his coffeecup on the table beside the divan and hoisted himself to his feet. "Well, I'd better get on to work." He turned to Mother. "Why don't you take the night off? Do you good."

"And leave you shorthanded? Goodness, no. The sooner we forget about all this, the better."

Don grinned down at her. "Okay. Whatever you think. Don't get up. I can find my way out." At the door he turned back. "Take it easy today. All of you. And

142

Louise, don't forget what we talked about, huh?"

Mother nodded, and Don's beefy hand gave a parting wave before he let himself out.

When the door closed behind him, I said to Mother, "What aren't you supposed to forget?"

"Oh, nothing," she said evasively. "Just something about work."

I accepted the answer. More important problems filled my mind. "Mother, when I called you about Keith last night, I don't see why you had to call on Don."

"Bernadette, there wasn't anyone else I *could* call on. Besides, Don knows so many of the men in the sheriff's department. And he was right there when you called. Not only that, he offered."

"Oh, for Pete's sake," Keith said wearily, "I didn't need anyone to get me out. No matter who was there, it wouldn't have made any difference."

Mother started to pull at her wisps of hair. "Just the same, Keith, it was nice of Don to help. I don't know what I would have done if he hadn't gone along with me—I was so *nervous*. And then he sent me home and took over and—well, I just don't know what I would have done without him."

Keith's blue eyes softened. "Sure, Louise. It was a lousy deal for you. I didn't mean it the way it sounded. It was nice of Don to take the trouble. He did a lot."

Mother looked mollified. Then she gave a long sigh. "Bernadette—Keith—there's a reason why I asked

143

Don." She placed her cup on the coffee table and gripped her hands together as if the act steadied her. "I wasn't going to tell you right now, but maybe this is as good a time as any. I asked Don—or rather, he offered be-cause—well, he has an—an interest. I mean—what I mean is, if he's going to be—" Her chin quivered. "Well, Don and I are thinking about getting married."

"Married!" Keith and I exclaimed together.

"Yes. I thought—we thought—well, we may be get-ting married."

"You've got to be kidding," Keith said.

My eyes started to fill. "How could you do this to us? How *could* you? You said you never would."

Keith sprang to his feet. "Well, don't expect me to live with you."

"Me neither. I'll go live with Gran."

The anxious expression on Mother's face changed to one of stubbornness. "I don't think you're being at all fair."

I said, "It's not that I mind the idea of your getting married someday, but not to just anyone."

"Don isn't just anyone. He—he's been so good. Be-sides, I—" She broke off.

Keith sat down again. He leaned forward and clasped his hands together between spread knees. Sounding very serious, he said, "Louise, I know what you're doing. You think because of what happened with this police business that we need someone older around to protect

144

us. You're wrong, Louise. You don't have to sacrifice yourself for us. We—"

I interrupted. "Oh, no, Mother. Please don't sacrifice yourself for us. We'll be okay. Everything will be okay. You'll see."

"If it's money," Keith said, "I can always quit school and get a job. There are plenty of things I can do."

Mother's shoulders sagged, and her blue eyes turned a dull gray. In a small voice that was almost apologetic, she said, "Did it ever occur to either of you that I might be in love with Don?"

Appalled, I murmured, "Oh, no—"

Keith said, "But you loved Dad! How could you love someone else now?"

Wordless, she slowly shook her head from side to side as if she had already accused herself of the same sin.

"You never loved Dad, did you?" Keith demanded, then answered his own question. "You couldn't have. If you didn't love him, then you don't care about me either."

"Oh, Keith, that's not true, and you know it! You're kids, both of you. You can't possibly understand something like this. Besides, I resent your trying to interfere."

I paid no attention to her words. "If you loved us, you wouldn't wreck our lives like this. That's what it'll do, you know. It'll wreck our lives."

Mother sighed deeply. I might have felt sorry for her except that I was hurting so badly. Her eyes glistened with unshed tears. "Oh, you don't understand. I never wanted to—well, I wouldn't do anything to hurt you, either one of you. And I do love you—both of you. You know I do." She chewed on her lower lip for a moment; then she rose and straightened her shoulders. "Let's not talk about it anymore. I told you once that I would never do anything that would make either one of you unhappy."

"Then you won't marry Don," I said.

Sounding tired, she said, "Right now, I don't know what I'll do. I'll have to think about it."

Keith said, "Good. Then you'll see that we're right."

Mother pursed her lips. "I don't want to talk about it anymore." She busied herself picking up coffeecups, then hastily went to the kitchen.

I guess we must have realized how much we'd upset her, because we both exchanged worried glances.

"She could never be happy with a guy like Don," Keith said, half to himself, half to me. "I mean, he's so—well, run-of-the-mill. What's he got outside a few restaurants?" He shook his head. "Louise shows signs of the dependency syndrome. She reminds me a little of Blanche in *A Streetcar Named Desire*. Louise is depending on the 'kindness of strangers.' Of course, Blanche was crazy and Louise isn't. She just has a need to lean on men too much."

He feels guilty because she can't lean on him, I thought. "Don't blame yourself, Keith. You're right. Everything will turn out for the best, you'll see. Someday Mother will thank us for keeping her from making a terrible mistake."

"I wasn't blaming myself. I wasn't blaming anybody. I just don't understand why—" Keith's words were lost in the shrill of the telephone.

I waited for Mother to pick it up in the kitchen. When the persistent ringing continued, I hurried out to answer it myself.

"Is Keith there?" a woman's voice asked.

"I'll call him," I said. No sooner had I laid down the receiver than it hit me. Giselle. If only my mind had been less of a jumble, I would have recognized her voice immediately and said, "Keith's not here." I stomped back into the living room and said in my most contemptuous voice, "It's for you—Giselle."

He stared up at me with a blank look.

"You know—the one who's just a friend."

His face reddened, but he got right up and with a few long strides vanished through the kitchen door.

"You don't have to run," I said disgustedly, although he was already out of hearing range. I sank down on the divan and tears stung my eyes.

That night, after Keith left for Giselle's apartment, I went into my bedroom and pulled out my pentagram.

Why wasn't it working? What had gone wrong? All I'd ever wanted was the power to control my future and my family's, the power to make things come out the way they should. In spite of my pentagram, in spite of all I had dared by using it for the sake of my family, everything was still taking off on its own. Obviously my concentration just wasn't good enough. I wasn't getting through. If you could not conjure up the demon you called upon, you had to work yourself up to a higher pitch and say the incantation in a fiercer and more commanding tone. I promised myself that I would try again that night, right after Mother had gone to work.

I went into her bedroom, where she was changing. She said, "Keith said he'll be right back, Bernadette. You won't have to stay alone long."

"I'm not worried about staying alone. But I *am* worried about *him*. Do you know where he's gone?"

"To see a friend, he said."

"The friend just happens to be Giselle Fox."

"The young woman who works in Eva's shop?"

"Yes. And in case you don't know, Keith's just plain silly about her. What's more, she's years and years older than he is."

Mother stopped what she was doing and stared at me. "Keith in love . . . are you sure?"

"I'm sure he thinks he is."

I was surprised to see a small smile playing at the corners of her mouth. "I can hardly believe it. He's never shown serious interest in any special girl before. In fact, I've been worried about him. Ever since Ralph's accident, he's seemed to keep himself at a distance from everybody."

"Well, what are you going to do about it?" I demanded.

"Do about it?" She laughed. "I'm not going to do anything about it. Keith is a young man now, not a child. He has a right to make his own choices in friends or in girlfriends."

"But she's so much older, and she's divorced and has kids."

Mother shook her head in a way that made me feel terribly naive. "Love is very seldom rational."

"Then you're not going to do anything?"

"Of course not. I trust Keith, and I think he's old enough to make his own mistakes and learn by them."

Talking about love brought to mind what she'd said earlier. "You're not *really* in love with Don, are you?"

She sighed. "I've been thinking about our talk tonight and about you and Keith and how you feel about things. I don't want to hurt either of you, but have you thought about how you might be hurting me?"

"Oh, Mother—we wouldn't do anything to hurt you ever. We just want what's best for you."

"Then, to answer your question, yes, I am in love with Don—deeply."

I felt sick. "But what about Ralph?"

"Honey, you can love more than one person in a lifetime. I loved your father, and I loved Ralph. I think it's *because* I loved them that I have the capacity to love someone else now. I mean, I know how satisfying it can be to share your life with another person, so I'm willing to try it again."

"But you have Keith and me to share your life with."

"Now didn't you just get through telling me that Keith is in love himself? He has his own life to live, and so do you. I'd be a bad mother if I expected you to sacrifice yourselves for me."

"Does that mean you're going to marry Don?"

She gave a weary sigh. "It means I'm thinking about it."

I fought back the tears, but said nothing. What was there to say? I was certain that Mother had already made up her mind, and if she had, there was no way Keith or I could ask her to change it. If she really loved Don, that wouldn't be fair to her.

But what if she didn't love Don? What if something changed her mind? Like my pentagram. If I could only call up Astaroth, that could change everything.

After Mother went to work, I took out my pentagram again, unfolded it, placed it on the floor, and stood in the middle. Again I went through the incantation that I had used before. When nothing happened, I repeated it over and over, working myself up to a higher pitch. Finally I said the words I'd been saving until last, words

I'd copied out of a book on the black arts that I'd seen in the shop. "O Astaroth, I command you to appear by the seven secret names with which Solomon controlled all demons"—I pronounced each one slowly and clearly—"Adonai. Perai. Tetragrammaton. Anexhexeton. Inessensatoal. Pathumaton. And Itemon. I threaten you by Eve, by Saray, by the name Primematum, which binds the whole host of heaven, to curse you, Astaroth, and hurl you into the bottomless pit, the lake of eternal fire, the lake of fire and brimstone, to remain there until the sounding of the last trumpet. Come, therefore, in the holy names Adonai, Zebaoth, Amioram. Come, Adonai commands you."

I said the last with all the energy and force I had; then I fell quiet and listened. A moment later I heard the sound of a heavy vehicle coming up our street. As it passed our house, the very walls seemed to shake and the windows shuddered. A sign. I had summoned up the demon, and now he had to do my bidding.

12

Keith parked near Giselle's apartment and sat in the car awhile, thinking about what he would say to her. He would forgive her, of course, would tell her he understood why she had told the police. Then, when he eventually left, he'd say in a cool, unemotional voice, "So long, Giselle. See you around." His imagined mastery of the situation made him feel good. He swung out of the car, closed the door with a smart clap, and headed up the street.

As he approached the apartment, he heard the front door slam and saw a skinny dark boy running down the few entry stairs. The kid stopped at the sidewalk, glanced at Keith, then turned away and shuffled off toward the alley that went back to the apartment car stalls. Another of the funky creeps who lived there, Keith thought.

As he entered the building, Sammy stuck his head out the door of his first-floor apartment and glanced up and down as if investigating a strange noise. When he spotted Keith, he gave a halfhearted nod and quickly ducked back inside. Keith knew Sammy slightly from happening upon him in Giselle's place so often and had long ago decided that Sammy's buttons, if not actually missing, were only hanging by threads.

Through glass panels in the front door, early twilight cast eerie bluish rays up the staircase as Keith ascended. His earlier feeling of assurance faded into gloom. By the time he reached Giselle's apartment, depression had set in.

Her door was ajar, but still he knocked instead of calling her name as he had once done. From someplace inside he heard her come running, flying. As she flung open the door, she called, "Keith, is it you?"

He melted at the sight of her. She was so pretty. Her dark hair was worn long and straight, the way he liked it, and golden hoops hung from her ears. Although she had dressed conventionally again tonight in skirt and sweater, he noticed a tiny crab painted on her cheek near her eye. Usually she wore a sun sign beauty mark only when she entertained. "Party?" he asked.

Her hand followed his glance to her cheek to touch the mark. "The crab is the Cancer sign. I'm trying to feel like a Cancer, because I have an appointment with a woman tonight, and that sign is more compatible with hers than my own."

Although he was glad to hear her appointment was with a woman, he was still disappointed. He found now that he wanted nothing more than enough time to talk to her and straighten out their relationship. "Can't you break the appointment?" he asked.

She looked at him strangely. "No, I really can't. It's important. You see, I'm consulting this woman about— well, about a problem I have."

"A psychiatrist?"

"No. Not exactly, but something like that."

A psychologist, he supposed. Although curious, he felt he had no right to pursue so personal a subject. After all, therapy was always confidential.

"The appointment isn't until later," she said, and led him into the room.

Keith sat down on the divan, stiffly tense, holding tight to his bitterness for fear it would vanish with the lull of her soft voice. Giselle sank down near him on an old plastic hassock and clasped her hands around her knees. She looked like an innocent little girl, he thought.

"Keith, why didn't you come right away when I called?"

"I—I couldn't." He wanted to lie, to say he had been too busy, but the words wouldn't come. "I just had to get some things straight in my head first."

Giselle stared at him for a long moment. Then she said, "And did you?"

"Yes."

"Want to tell me about it?"

Now was the time for all the rehearsed words. "It doesn't really matter, Giselle. You had to do what you did, I suppose. I can't really—"

"Keith, I didn't."

"I really can't blame you. After all, I told you to go ahead and—"

"Keith, will you listen to me? I didn't tell anybody—not in the way you think, anyhow."

He was so set on finishing his prepared speech, he had trouble grasping her words. "You didn't?"

"No. That's why I asked you to come over. I knew what you'd think, and it wasn't true. I never said a word, Keith. It was Sammy. And you mustn't hate him for it."

There was no room in Keith's heart to hate anyone. Instead, a great joy surged through him. Like church bells ringing out a hymn on Sunday morning, the words, over and over, rang in his heart: *It was not Giselle, it was not Giselle. Joy to the world!*

"They've been questioning everyone who hangs around the shop," Giselle said. "I don't think Sammy would have even remembered when it was—he's not much on dates—but they kept hammering at him to account for that night. It seems there was some longshoremen's thing he went to. When he remembered that, he remembered seeing you with Francine at the same time he was leaving for it."

155

Now it came back to Keith. When he had slammed out of the apartment with Francine that Friday night, he had almost bumped into Sammy. He'd been so angry, he had hardly noticed the guy.

"After they questioned Sammy," Giselle continued, "they talked to me again. You know, they'd talked to me once before. I never even mentioned you then, Keith—not a word. This time they asked me why I hadn't told them you'd taken Francine home that night. I told them I just didn't remember what night it was— still didn't. After all, it happened on a Friday and she wasn't found until Sunday. It's hard to remember what went on, even a couple of days ago."

"Why didn't you tell them, Giselle? I mean, in the first place."

Giselle was thoughtful for a moment. "I—I had to trust my own feelings."

"ESP feelings?"

She dimpled. "Maybe." Then she grew serious again. "I never believed you had anything to do with it, Keith. And I never once asked the cards. It would have been like doubting you. I had to go on my own feelings. And, you see, I was right—else you wouldn't be here now, would you?" She tossed her head, setting the golden hoops at her ears dancing. Her eyes avoided his as she unclasped her hands from around her knees to reach for and fidget with a box of matches on the coffee table. Finally, she struck one and absorbed herself in lighting

156

a fat red candle that sat in its own puddle of wax.

Keith watched in fascination as the candle flame leaped to her earrings, a reflected fire, locked in for a moment to make them blaze like fiery hoops in a circus. He felt himself brazenly plunging through. "Why didn't you tell them about me?" he repeated in a tone that demanded the truth.

She put down the matches and folded her hands quietly in her lap. The earrings ceased to blaze, and became shiny gold again, dangling soberly from her tiny ears. "It hassled me for a while, Keith." She frowned. "I wasn't sure of anything except what I felt. Then, after a time, it all came clear—like a revelation. And it was all so simple—there was no problem at all. You just don't cop out on people you love. You can't."

Keith's heart started to hammer in his chest. He swallowed what seemed like a great lump in his throat. "You love everyone, Giselle," he said softly.

"Is that what you think?"

"Well, *don't* you?"

"Maybe I do—but there are degrees."

"Where does that leave me?"

Her eyes shifted to her hands. "You have a very special place, Keith. I care about what happens to you."

"That doesn't sound very special."

She looked up and mimicked the dark expression on his face, then smiled. "You're looking angry again."

157

"I'm not angry," he protested, yet scowled more deeply.

Her eyes looked a little sad. "What is it you want from me?"

He stifled an urge to reach out and touch her. Instead, he blurted, "I want you to—to care about me the way I care about you."

She gave a little sigh. "I'm much older than you, Keith."

"Seven years. Big deal."

"Seven years is a lot."

"It doesn't have to matter."

"But it can."

"Only if *you* let it."

"In four more years I'll be thirty years old. You'll only be twenty-three."

"Why do we have to think in terms of years—four more years, five more years, ten more years? Why can't we just think of now?"

"Keith, I just don't know."

She sounded as if she was weakening. His heart took a quick bound. He leaned forward and awkwardly reached for her hand, so small, so like a child's with square little fingers and unpolished nails that looked chewed. He felt oddly touched as he stroked it. "Giselle . . . let me love you."

At length she drew her hand away and, with a bewildered expression in her eyes, absently touched the area his fingers had stroked. Then she got quickly to her feet. "Oh, Keith, I don't know . . . I can't think . . . and I have to go out in a few minutes." She glanced wildly around as if seeking the answer in some other part of the apartment. In the tarot cards tucked away in a drawer? In some crystal ball sitting on a table in another room? "Besides," she added, "I think I'll know what's right by the time I come back."

Did that mean she was seeing someone about him? The thought gave him hope. He pressed what he instinctively recognized as his advantage. He sprang forward and gripped her shoulders. His voice trembled. "Giselle . . . I love you. . . ."

"Keith, let me think about it a little."

He stiffened. "I see."

"I didn't mean it that way. I mean, I think we should talk it out, and there just isn't time now."

"Talk—what good would that do? Giselle, don't you think you could care for me—even a little?"

"I already care for you, Keith. Too much, I think."

He pulled her into his arms and locked her to him, burying his nose in her hair. He could smell a spicy perfume that made his pulses quicken. Finally, she pulled free. "You've got to let me go," she said. "I've got a fairly long drive ahead of me."

"Can I see you soon? Later tonight—after your appointment?"

"It'll be too late."

159

"That's all right."

She laughed. "Oh, all right. But just for a little while. Sometime after eleven."

He was still in a daze when she led him to the door and opened it. She pointed to the tiny drawing on her cheek. "There's another reason why I want to feel like a Cancer tonight."

"Why?"

"Because Cancer people are steadfast."

He smiled down at her, love warming his heart, melting away the cold winter so long a part of him. She reached up and gently touched his cheek. Then she pulled his head down to hers and her lips brushed his in a quick, tender kiss. Before he could respond, she pushed him firmly out the door.

Was it only a few hours before that he had felt so deeply upset about Louise and Don? Now their relationship no longer seemed to matter. Nor did his vow to never get close to another human being. Now he floated on a cushion of air, a buoyant ocean of love.

As he drove home, he thought about Louise and Don. Somehow you never really considered it possible for older people to fall in love. Did they feel the way he felt at that moment, or was it different for them? He wondered now if he hadn't come on a bit heavy with Louise, telling her off the way he had. Did he have any right to tell her how to live her life, even if what she did affected his?

Besides, he suspected that, all along, he'd been unfair to Don. In many ways, he had to admit, Don was a lot like his father. In fact, after Keith's bout with the police, when they had been driving home, Don had even sounded like his father.

"What do you know about that shop where your sister was learning how to tell fortunes?" he had asked.

"Not very much," Keith said. "I guess a lot of occultist types hang out there."

"Well, I've been talking to one of the sheriff's boys. He says that that kind of stuff often attracts sick minds. He says it's a great outlet for perversion. Now, I don't know too much about these things, but he seems to think that your sister's friend's killer could be someone who spends time in that shop. Whether that's the case or not, I think you should try to persuade Bernadette to stay away from the place."

Although Keith wanted to resent what he suspected was fatherly advice, he had to admit that the sheriff's suspicions made the suggestion a reasonable one. "I'll tell her," he had said. Then Giselle's call had driven everything else from his mind. Now he decided to tell Bernadette immediately and, later tonight, when he saw Giselle, he would warn her, too.

13

I had just finished the incantation to send Astaroth back when I heard the sound of a VW engine in the driveway. Keith. I was glad of that. Fooling with black magic really frightened me. The danger in trying to control demons was that one false step and they would control you. While I was relieved that Keith hadn't returned in time to catch me in the act, I needed someone else in the house now to drive out the terror I was beginning to feel.

When he called my name, I closed my bedroom door hastily, afraid he might smell the candles I'd had burning, and joined him in the living room.

"Listen," he said, "I forgot to mention to you. This afternoon Don said that the police think Francine's killer might be someone who hangs around in her mother's shop. Now, I know you haven't been back to that tarot class, but what about afternoons? You don't go there anymore, do you?"

I certainly wasn't going to tell him about visiting Giselle there to check up on him. "Of course not."

"Good. You just stay away from the place."

"Don't worry." The shop held too many sad memories now. "Keith," I said, changing the subject, "Mother told me tonight that she's in love with Don. She said *deeply*."

He stared at me for a long moment before he said, "Is she going to marry him?"

"She says she's thinking about it. Keith, we've got to stop her."

"And how do you think we can do that?"

"I thought maybe if we both concentrated hard on her hating Don. I mean, really visualized it in our heads, then maybe we could will it to happen." Having his mind work on the problem along with mine couldn't hurt.

To my surprise, he shook his head disparagingly. "I think I know what you have in mind. And in some cases it might even work. The human mind and will and imagination are potent instruments."

I broke in, "Oh, yes." I thought of the tarot cards— The Magician representing the human will, The High Priestess representing enlightenment, The Empress representing action—and of Giselle's story about the two men behind prison bars and how one looked out and saw mud while the other saw stars. I found myself repeating her words: "Things are the way you see them."

His eyes rested on me thoughtfully before he said, "Not always, Bernadette. Sometimes there are limits to what the human mind and will can accomplish. Sometimes, above and beyond the way you see things is something else—the way things really are. Above and beyond what you wish for is what is possible for you to have."

"I don't believe that. I think there are ways to make your wishes come true. You just have to learn how to focus your mind and will. You can use charms or crystal balls or a lot of things to do it." I didn't mention my pentagram, because I knew he wouldn't understand a thing like that.

"I see. You're talking about magic." He gave a deep sigh. "Bunny, Bunny, what are we going to do with you? I know someone else who's just like you."

I knew immediately who the someone was.

"Don't you think it would be more sensible to develop your mind to act without the need for charms and such? Isn't it more satisfying to know that you've accomplished a goal with your own abilities? Depending upon charms can destroy your faith in yourself, your confidence. Can't you understand that?"

"I don't know what you mean," I said, feeling stubborn.

164

"I mean that if you believe that by using magic you can gain control of the will of others, then you, too, become a victim of that same magic."

"I don't understand."

"I mean you become psychologically vulnerable to magic. You start to live in fear that someone else will try to control *your* mind, *your* will. Anyone who believes he can cause illness in someone else by sticking pins in wax images is the first to waste away at the fear that someone might be doing the same thing to him. People don't control magic. Magic always controls them."

The way Keith said the words frightened me, especially because it was black magic I was playing with. "If I'm not supposed to use magic, then what are we going to do about Don?"

"You know, I don't think there's anything we *can* do about him except make the best of the situation. I know you can't realize how your mother feels because you've never felt that way yourself. I think I understand better now. If she really loves Don, that isn't something she can turn off because we ask her to."

I said despairingly, "It's not Don so much. Oh, I just want to go back home."

He looked at me as if he wasn't sure of how to deal with me now. "Oh, Bunny, you don't really want to go back to Willow Orchard. You want to go back to the nice life we once knew when Dad was alive. You can't. It just isn't there anymore for any of us. All we can do now is go on from here and try to make another life that's as good in its own way as the old one."

A little while before he had been raging at Mother, saying that he wouldn't live with her if she married Don, and now he seemed to have swallowed the possibility whole. What had changed him so suddenly? Surely not that short visit with Giselle. Or had it? And was he right about Willow Orchard? I felt so confused.

"But life here isn't as good as it was back there. That's the trouble. Mother's different, and so are you," I said.

"I'm not different."

"Oh, yes, you are, Keith. Ever since Ralph died, you've been like someone I don't even know."

He looked as if he was going to deny the accusation, then surprised me by saying, "I guess I have been short with you at times, but I didn't really mean to be."

"It's not that. I don't mind about that. It's just that back there I used to feel as though you cared about me. We used to talk about things. We were so much closer."

"But there just isn't time now."

"I don't believe that's it at all. Now that I think about it, it started before we ever came out here. It started right after Ralph died. What happened to you then?"

His eyes narrowed. "You know I don't like to talk about that."

"I know that you *won't* talk about it." I sat down on the sofa, crossed my arms, and stared at him hard.

"That's not really the case."

"I think it is. And you know what else I think? I think that for some reason you blame yourself for his

166

death." I had wanted to say that to him for a long time, and until now I hadn't dared. Maybe I was afraid that the truth was something I wouldn't want to hear. "What happened that day, Keith?"

I could see him stiffen. "You know what happened. Everybody knows."

I waited in silence to see if he would say anything else. At length he said, "Of course I don't blame myself. Louise was there. She'd tell you that there wasn't anything we could do. It happened just as we got there. You know that."

"I also know that there's more to it than you're telling me."

He said nothing and neither did I. When the silence lengthened, I felt that that was all I was going to get out of him. Suddenly, sounding as if he were talking to himself, he said, "Strange. Now that I think of it, someone else once asked me if I felt guilty about Dad's death. She said that when I talked about it, I had a certain look on my face that made her wonder."

I felt a prickle of annoyance. "I suppose you're talking about Giselle."

"As a matter of fact, yes. I told her what happened to Dad, and that was her reaction."

"What would she know about something like that?" I said sarcastically.

He sounded defensive. "She has a great deal of insight into people."

"But you just said you don't blame yourself. If she

167

said you do, I wouldn't call that insight."

He looked thoughtful. "Sometimes other people see something in you that you don't see in yourself. Too often, we tend to lie to ourselves."

I felt a little jealous to realize that Giselle must have struck a chord in him that I never could. "Is that what you've been doing, then—lying to yourself?"

He stared off into space. "I never thought so." He was quiet for a long time, as if figuring out something in his own mind. Finally he said softly, "But why does it keep eating away at my gut?" He sounded as if he was experiencing some kind of revelation. "Why do I keep telling myself that I should never have reminded her—"

"Reminded her?"

He glanced over to me with a look that suggested he had forgotten I was there. "I mean about the shirt. You remember how Louise and I were supposed to pick up Dad that afternoon?" As he talked, he started pacing the room.

I nodded.

"Well, I was the one who reminded her that he'd be dirty. You know how Dad was. He could never be around a job without pitching in. She was a little late anyhow, but she went back into the house for a clean shirt. And that was all it took—those few extra minutes—that damned shirt."

"Then you do blame yourself!"

He stopped pacing and shrugged. "I never thought I

did. Yet I must have, or else that idea couldn't keep bothering me the way it does."

"You mean, all this time you had all that guilt inside you and you didn't even know it?"

"Oh, I guess I knew it all right—on a certain level. You always do, even when your conscious self denies it."

"You're the one who's always saying that denial is not a healthy way of dealing with repressed emotions."

"Am I always saying that? Well, I'm right. Maybe I've been denying how guilty I felt about Dad's death, but believe me, I've been pretty honest with myself about my mother's."

"Your mother's! She died of a ruptured appendix. What could you possibly have to do with that?"

"I know, but she died so soon after my birth—three weeks. It makes you wonder."

"I don't see why."

"Neither did I until Dad was killed. Then, for some reason, I started thinking about her death and wondering why the people closest to me had to die."

"You mean, like you have some kind of a jinx?"

He shrugged. "I suppose you could put it that way."

"And you think *I'm* superstitious!"

"Oh, I keep telling myself that I don't really believe any of those things, but someplace, deep inside, I do. As much as I try to deny it, the thought keeps eating at me."

All I could say was, "Oh, boy, Keith, if someone

you knew told you what you've just told me, what would you say to them?"

He gave a wry smile. "I'd say, 'Man, you're laying a guilt trip on yourself you don't deserve!' "

"I just can't get over you, Keith! How can you know so much about what makes everybody else tick and yet not see what you're doing to yourself?"

"It's not intellectual, it's emotional. You can't think yourself out of your feelings."

"Oh, no? Well, you just better try. You said Mother was a little late that afternoon. You said it was her idea to run back into the house for a clean shirt. That makes her more guilty than you."

"But *I* was the one who reminded her that he'd be dirty."

"But you weren't the one who made her late in the first place. By your thinking, that should make her guilty of Ralph's death."

"Of course it doesn't. Don't you suppose I know that?"

"Then why don't you know you're not guilty either?"

"Because knowing it intellectually isn't the same as knowing it emotionally. No matter how hard I try not to think about those things, someplace deep inside me I keep asking myself if I was a good enough son to Dad while he was alive, and the answer is always no. Then I wonder about my mother. What if I'd never been born? Would she still be alive?"

"Wow, Keith, you could drive yourself crazy with silly ideas like that."

"I know."

"Well, at least you've admitted how you feel. You never did that before."

He looked almost sheepish. "You're right. Who knows? Maybe now that I've faced the fact that I do feel that way, I'll be able to deal with it better."

"Just remember that if you can let Mother off the hook, you should be able to let yourself off, too."

He looked at me and grinned. "How'd you get so smart all of a sudden?"

I grinned back, feeling that this was more like the old days, when we used to talk about things that were important, things that brought us closer together.

His expression made me think he was remembering and sharing my thoughts. He said, "I do care about you, Bunny. You couldn't be a better sister if you were a blood sister. If I haven't been much of a brother lately, I'm really sorry. I'll try to make it up to you from now on."

"I'll hold you to that." He sat down on the sofa beside me and gave me a big hug. We both smiled, and it seemed as if the nice warm feeling that we used to have between us had returned. I had been coming to believe that he didn't like me anymore. Now I was reassured. If I was hurting because the old life had vanished, so was he. Worse, a part of him had blamed himself.

171

14

Keith, excited and full of hope, bounded up the steps to Giselle's apartment. The hour was well after eleven. He had deliberately given her more than enough time to keep her appointment and return home. Delaying the encounter allowed him to prolong his anticipation of her answer, which was sure to be yes. It was only as he neared her door and spotted the envelope taped to it, his name on it, that he had his first indication that something was amiss. Giselle had obviously been there and gone. Why?

He stared at the envelope for a long moment, afraid to read what she had written. At the same time his mind was busy making all kinds of excuses for her. She had been called away for some emergency. Perhaps one of her children was sick. Or her mother.

Finally, with unsteady hands, he grabbed the envelope. As he pulled it off, he was surprised to feel the door move. Giselle hadn't even taken a moment to close and lock it. What could have compelled her to rush off like that? Feeling uneasy, he tore open her note.

I'm going away for a few days, it read. *I've arranged it with Eva in the shop, and I want to be gone before you get here. I don't think we should see each other again. After my appointment I realized how mixed up my head was. It wouldn't work, she said.*

Keith could not bring himself to read on. Was it only minutes ago that he'd felt so happy? Shoulders drooping, he turned to leave. Then the thought occurred to him that perhaps she was hiding inside. Yes, that had to be it. That was why she hadn't locked the door. And the fact that she hadn't closed it tightly could be a subconscious wish for him to find and reason with her.

More hopeful now, he pushed it open and entered, not at all prepared for the horror that awaited him inside.

15

I lay on my bed, staring up at the ceiling but seeing nothing. I still couldn't believe it. Last night Giselle had been murdered and Keith was being held for questioning. And I suspected that it was all my fault. The guilt made me feel wasted.

All along I had known about the dangers in calling up demons, but I had had to go ahead anyhow. All the books warned that you might not be able to control them, but I hadn't listened. Now it was too late to undo the evil I had done.

Why, I wondered, hadn't I made the connection sooner? The first time I'd used the incantations was the night the hitchhiker was murdered. The second time was the night of Francine's murder. Last night I'd used them again and Giselle was murdered. I wanted to believe coincidence was responsible, but I couldn't. This had all happened because I'd tried to interfere with other people's destinies.

In the late afternoon the doorbell rang, and I assumed Mother, who had gone to see about Keith, had returned and forgotten her key. I pulled myself up and hurried to the front door, hoping to see Keith with her. Instead of Mother and Keith, the caller was Don.

"Oh, it's you," I said.

"Your mother left a message for me at the restaurant—something about Keith. Is she here?" he asked, stepping inside the door.

"No."

"Is Keith in trouble?"

I hesitated, wondering if I should tell him the awful news. Then I decided that if he was really in love with Mother, he'd want to do anything he could to spare her pain. Then, too, he'd helped Keith before. Perhaps he'd help him again. "He's being held for questioning in a woman's murder, and Mother's gone down to see what it's all about."

He frowned. "Another murder?" he murmured, almost to himself. "Who was the woman?"

"Her name is"—I corrected myself—"was Giselle Fox. She worked at The Mandrake Root."

"Isn't that the shop that's owned by the parents of the other girl who was murdered?"

"Yes."

"Why are they holding Keith?"

"He was found in her apartment with her"—I shuddered—"with her dead body."

"Who found him?"

"S-Sammy," I said in a stutter that sounded as if my teeth were chattering. "He found him in Giselle's apartment. He—he called the police. They came and got Keith."

"Who's Sammy?"

"Sammy Rupp—he lives downstairs. He—he's a psychic. He and Giselle are friends." I could feel tears well up in my eyes. "I mean, they were."

He nodded gravely. "I wonder if it's made the papers yet."

"I don't know."

He glanced at his wristwatch, then at me. "I'm going to find out. I'll be back in five minutes or so. Then I'd like to ask you some more questions. Oh, and I could use a cup of coffee if it's not too much trouble."

"It's okay," I said, and he hurried off to disappear out the front door.

By the time he returned, I had the coffeepot on the stove and cups and saucers set out on the pass-through bar. Don, the afternoon edition tucked under his arm, joined me in the kitchen. He opened the paper and scanned the front page. I glanced over his shoulder to see Giselle's face smiling up at me. The radiance that

176

lived only in a photograph now gave me a cold sick feeling in the pit of my stomach. Don said, "They found Keith in the apartment in a state of shock, it says. I wonder what he was doing there and why he didn't report the crime to the police."

I turned away and busied myself carrying the cups into the living room. Horrible thoughts, like crawly insects, wanted to push up out of some dark corner of my mind, but I kept shoving them back.

He read on and said, "Apparently he had a note on him that she'd written. They're not giving out the contents, but they intimate that he was a rejected suitor. No wonder they suspect him."

Don carried the paper into the living room, tossed it onto the divan, and sat down. I got the coffeepot and filled his cup. When he picked up and opened the paper, instead of reading it he stared off into space and mused, "I hire a lot of people in my business, and I like to think I'm a pretty good judge of character. So far, very few of them have disappointed me. It's my opinion that Keith could never commit a crime of this sort."

I felt a vague stirring within. "You don't think so?"

"Of course not. And I'm sure you don't think so either."

"Oh, no," I said too quickly.

"And if Keith didn't commit those crimes, someone else did."

I nodded, although I wasn't really convinced. "If only there were some way to find out who it is."

"Well, so far the police haven't done much good. I don't see how we could do much worse."

"You mean *we* should look for the murderer?"

"Maybe not that exactly, but two of the victims were connected with that shop in The Village. Your mother tells me you used to spend a lot of time there. Maybe you know something the police don't. What about this fellow Sammy Rupp they mention in the paper?"

"Oh, not Sammy," I murmured. In an instant, shame filled me again. What a monster I was. I was ready to believe Sammy innocent when I had just as readily judged Keith guilty. To make up for it, I told Don everything I knew about Sammy, even to the nude pinup on the closet door.

Don listened solemnly. When I finished, he said, "He's certainly a possibility." He picked up the newspaper, and his eyes searched the front page. Another item seemed to capture his interest. After a moment he asked, "Have you ever heard of an Olivia Remy?"

"Yes. She lives out on the Peninsula. Everyone calls her a witch."

"Including the lady herself, evidently." He read from the article: " 'Olivia Remy, the Peninsula's official witch, claims she can tell police the identity of the killer. However, when questioned about Miss Remy's offer, local police took a dim view of her psychic evidence.' " Don shook his head disgustedly and tossed the paper back on the divan.

I looked at him anxiously. "Maybe she *does* know something." I knew that no matter what the people in Eva's shop said about her, she was the one they all consulted when there was something important they wanted to find out.

"As far as I can see, psychics have been trying to horn in on murder cases for years. If this woman had any real evidence, she would run with it to the police. It would give her the publicity she obviously craves. No, it's not psychics who'll find our killer."

I nodded and shifted my eyes down to our worn rug. I wasn't about to argue, but all the same, I had a very strong feeling about Olivia. People said she could give past-life readings and predict the future. Even Giselle, long ago, had told me that she'd once gone to her to get help for some problem about her children. If Olivia Remy said she knew who the killer was, she probably did.

My speculations were interrupted as Don said, "I think I'd better get down to the police station and see what the situation is with Keith. Maybe I can be of help."

The words made me feel so guilty. Don's was one of the destinies I'd been attempting to mess with. Now here he was, trying to help out when we really had no one else to turn to.

"Mother will appreciate anything you can do," I said.

He smiled at me and I noticed something about him I had never seen before. He had a very nice smile with even, white teeth.

After he left, I had a great deal to think about. Although Don didn't believe Keith had murdered anyone, all I could visualize was the blood on his face and his arm the night Francine was murdered. Would the police hold someone this long if they didn't have some strong evidence? I asked myself. The answer seemed all too obvious.

I went to my room and, out of my dresser drawer, took the pine box that held my tarot cards. Could they tell me what I needed to know? Up until now I'd really only played with them, trying to learn what each meant and how one related to the others. I'd never asked them anything important. But this was a desperate situation. I needed all the help I could get. If the cards told me Keith was not a murderer, what a load that would take off my mind.

I took them out of the box, shuffled them, cut them, and mentally asked them yes or no. Was he or wasn't he guilty? Afraid to find out, I closed my eyes and laid out five cards before me on the dresser top. When I finally forced myself to look, I gasped. The answer was yes. Keith was guilty, and in the cards I read his fate.

The first card, The Wheel of Fortune, is the rewards card. Next to it lay The Chariot, the card of aggression.

Then came Judgment, the card of trial. Because it was in the middle, it represented Keith. The Star followed, but it was upside down, so it meant loss of hope. And last, The Hierophant, the salvation card, was also upside down. There was only one way to read the layout. The reward or outcome of Keith's violent acts was trial (and that could be a legal trial) with no hope for salvation.

I stared at the cards for a long time. I thought of the Keith I had known back in Willow Orchard. That Keith could never have killed anyone. Then the conversation we had had only yesterday came flooding back into my mind. Why would he have been concerned about my hanging around the shop if he had been the murderer? And would someone who could murder savagely and in cold blood be capable of feeling guilt of any kind? No.

Yet the cards had declared him the murderer. Then I remembered that Giselle always said that when you read cards, you were looking into your own soul. Was it I, rather than the tarot, who had judged him? I remembered something else she'd said. "When you read the cards, it doesn't mean that things *have* to turn out the way the cards say. It means that up to now, the way things are going, if they keep on going the same way, that's the way they're bound to turn out unless you change them. And you *can* change them. It's all up to you."

All up to me.

The words were like a voice from the dead. I glanced at the cards again and saw how I could interpret them differently. They could be saying that even if Keith was innocent he would be tried and found guilty. As I studied them further, I discovered that I could read many other interpretations into them, too. How could I know which was right?

Your soul knows. Those were Giselle's words, too. Right now the only thing my soul knew was that in spite of anything the cards said, and whether or not I was reading them right, I believed in Keith's innocence.

I gathered up the cards and tossed them into their box and back into my drawer, almost certain I would never consult them again.

I thought back to the newspaper article about Olivia Remy. She had said she knew who the murderer was. The cards had said Keith. Would she say Keith, too? She had to know the police were questioning him.

None of the psychics who hung around the shop liked her, yet they still seemed to believe that she possessed a power greater than theirs. Even Giselle had consulted her. If only I could talk to the woman and find out what she knew. Was she, even now, planning to tell the police and the newspapers that Keith was the murderer? If so, I had to somehow convince her that she was wrong. I couldn't bear the idea of Keith shut away in some horrid prison. And there was an even worse possible fate these

182

days: execution. The thought was chilling.

I knew I couldn't just call up Olivia Remy and ask her what she knew; but if I could see her in person, I was sure I could somehow find out. There was only one way to accomplish that, so I went out to the kitchen and looked up her number in the phone book. She was listed under Spiritual Consultants. I dialed and was surprised to hear a male voice answer.

"Madame Remy's secretary speaking," he said.

I was expecting Olivia Remy to answer, so for a moment I was tongue-tied.

"Is anyone there?"

"Er—may I speak to—to Madame Remy?"

"She's engaged at the moment. Do you wish a consultation?"

"Well, er, yes."

"For a past-life reading?"

"No."

"What then?"

"I—er—well, I guess you could say a present-life reading."

"How old are you?" the voice demanded. "Madame doesn't do readings for children."

"I'm seventeen," I lied.

"Oh, I see. Well, you sound very young. I should tell you that on straight readings of a half hour, a donation of thirty-five dollars for PSI is requested."

I gulped, then said in a small voice, "PSI?"

183

"Psychic and Spiritualist Institute."

Whether or not Olivia Remy was psychic, her secretary must have been. How else could he have known that thirty-five dollars was the exact amount I'd saved toward Christmas gifts? "That will be okay. Can I get an appointment right away?"

"Right away?" he said, sounding as if I were asking the impossible. "You mean tonight?"

"Well, yes. Just as soon as possible."

"Well, I hardly think . . ." He paused, and I imagined he was studying some calendar. "Ah, you're in luck. Madame has a cancellation at six-thirty. Do you need directions to The Villa?"

"No. I know where it is."

"Good. Your name, please?"

I didn't want to give my real name, just in case. "Lisa," I said. "Lisa Johnson."

When I hung up, I congratulated myself. The whole thing had worked more easily than I'd dreamed. Then I thought about how some people insisted that Olivia Remy was a Satanist. If there was any truth in their belief, I would need a very strong amulet, indeed, to protect me.

But I had just discarded the cards in favor of acting on my own judgment. Would carrying an amulet with me be like depending on the cards? No, I told myself. Lots of people carried lucky charms. Even if they did no good, they could certainly do no harm.

184

16

The time was already five-thirty. I would have to hurry if I was to purchase the amulet I needed before heading for The Villa. I had no idea how often the buses ran, but I knew I could check at The Mandrake Root. Giselle always kept a schedule beneath the counter. I thought about her now as I approached the shop and, for the first time, fully realized that there would be no smiling Giselle to greet me there. Again guilt and grief overwhelmed me.

Inside the store Steve broke off his conversation with his only other customer, who, as it turned out, was Sammy. Both of them stared at me in a way that almost made me feel they had just been talking about me. Afraid that either one of them could read my thoughts if he wanted to, I tried to make my mind a blank and browse around the place like a casual customer.

"Sure am sorry about your brother, Bernadette," Sammy said as he plodded toward me.

I remembered bitterly that it was he who had turned Keith in. "Keith never murdered anyone," I blurted out, then realized how defensive I sounded.

In a stern voice, Steve said, "Nobody's accusing any-one—yet."

"I didn't mean nothin' like that, Bernadette. Honest," Sammy said, then blundered on. "Course, if'n he done it, most likely they won't kill him or nothin'—put him away someplace is all."

"Why are you not at home where you belong?" Steve asked, eyeing me suspiciously. "I would think your mother could use some comfort."

Now I knew I'd made a mistake coming here, yet I absolutely needed that amulet. I tried to sound scornful as I said, "Mother knows it's all a silly mistake. We're not a bit worried, either of us. They'll soon have the real murderer."

"Yeah?" Sammy murmured.

"Yes," I declared, firmly enough, I hoped, to give the impression that I knew what I was talking about.

At that moment I felt a draft of cold air and turned to see Mark Keeper enter the shop. He gave a quick nod toward Sammy and me and headed for the book-shelves, where he examined one of the books and began scribbling in a notebook.

I had more important things on my mind than Mark. If I was ever to get where I was going, I knew I couldn't waste any more time. I strode past Sammy and to the counter, where I fingered a bunch of amulets that hung pendantlike from chains. When I found the one I wanted, I said, "Oh, I really like this one," and handed it to Steve, trying to make it seem as if I were buying on impulse. Then in a low voice I asked him, "I wonder if I could see the bus schedule that—that is kept under the counter."

"What bus schedule?" he said impatiently. "We have no bus schedule here."

Still keeping my voice low, I persisted. "It was always kept right down there." I pointed to the area beneath the counter, from where Giselle had taken it to let Francine and me see it on the day we went out to the Peninsula.

Steve, a disgruntled frown on his face, rummaged around until he came upon a pamphlet, which he scrutinized, then handed to me. "This what you mean?"

It was open to the section that showed the Peninsula bus schedule. "Yes," I said, taking it from him. Apparently no one had even looked at it since the day Francine and I had used it. That gave me a funny feeling. I ran my eyes over it to discover that buses ran every hour on the hour. That meant there was one due at six o'clock. The ride, I remembered, took close to thirty minutes. The walk from Peninsula Drive up to The Villa probably took about fifteen more. I would be a little late, but there was nothing I could do about it.

As I returned the schedule to Steve, he asked rudely, "Why do you want to go out to the Peninsula?" His voice carried throughout the store.

I looked around and, to my dismay, saw Sammy and Mark both staring at me. I said to Steve, "I have a friend there."

He shrugged and glanced down at the amulet I'd handed him and removed the price tag. As he noticed what I'd chosen, he smiled. "Magic squares—a powerful amulet, this one. You know what it is?"

I tried to look ignorant. "I just thought it was kind of interesting looking."

He pointed to the numbered squares etched in copper. "You see here, the numbers go from one to thirty-six. If you add them all, they total six hundred and sixty-six. This is the Cabalist's magic square for the sun, a powerful, powerful force."

"Six sixty-six?" someone said.

I looked up to see Sammy beside me. Sammy said, "Lemme see that there amulet," and leaned his great bulk over the counter for a closer look.

"What's the matter?" Steve asked.

Sammy frowned at me. "Six sixty-six is the number of the Beast of Revelation, the Antichrist. You musta knowed that, Bernadette."

"No, I didn't know that," I lied. "Besides, I think

188

it's pretty, and as long as it's the sun square, I guess it doesn't matter about some beast." I paid Steve and, as quickly as I could, left the store.

Outside, I clasped the chain around my neck and hid the amulet under the sweater I was wearing. The reason I had chosen magic squares was that the life force of the sun was a power that could help me master my environment and survive, and I thought I might very well need that kind of power at Olivia Remy's, not knowing exactly what to expect there. I hurried up the street, aware of the darkening sky, aware of a foggy dampness creeping in.

I walked as far as the bus stop and sat on the bench there. A glance at my watch told me the time was ten of six. I wouldn't have too long to wait. Soon I heard heavy footsteps coming up the street toward me. I glanced around to find they belonged to Sammy. "Hey, Bernadette," he said, "you goin' out to the Peninsula?"

I saw no reason to lie. Lots of people lived out there. I could be going to see any one of them. "Yes, I am, Sammy."

"You really gotta go out there?"

I couldn't imagine what he was getting at. "Well, yes."

"You shouldn't be runnin' 'round by yourself at night, Bernadette. If'n you want, I'll get my car. Won't take but a minute. I'll drive you wheresoever you wanna go."

I remembered how Don had questioned me about Sammy. If Keith had had nothing to do with the murders, then the murderer *could* be Sammy. As much as I would have appreciated the ride, I just couldn't chance it. "It's okay, Sammy. Someone's meeting me at the bus."

"You sure?"

"Yes, I'm sure."

"Won't be no trouble, y'know."

His persistence frightened me. "Sammy, I have to take the bus. These people I'm going to see will be looking for me to come that way."

He shrugged. "Well, okay. See ya." He turned away and walked off.

As his footsteps faded into the distance, I felt just as relieved as if I'd really known he was the killer. What was wrong with me, anyhow? One minute I thought Keith was the guilty one. The next minute I wasn't sure of anything. The only thing I *was* sure of was that I had to find out what Olivia Remy knew. If anyone would know who had done the murders, a true psychic would.

There were only a few people on the bus when I boarded. I considered myself fortunate that it came right on time. All the way, I kept glancing at my watch and willing the bus to go faster, faster, but the fog was thickening now, so the driver had to take it easy. When I finally got off at the abandoned gatehouse beside the road to The Villa, I checked the time with the light

190

from the bus. Six twenty-five. If I ran some of the way, I wouldn't be too late.

The thought suddenly dawned on me that I hadn't left any kind of note for Mother. But what would I have said anyhow? That I'd gone to the library? I couldn't tell the truth, and anyone would know that you didn't do such things when your brother was in jail and you were waiting to find out the score. If Mother got home before me, she would just have to worry. I wouldn't be any longer than I had to be, anyhow.

I hurried past the gatehouse and up the road. A full moon helped light the way, even through the fog, probably because it was spottier here, dense in some areas while in others there was none at all. I ran as long as I could, but the road was all uphill, and winded, I soon had to give up to catch my breath.

After what seemed like ages, I finally saw a hazy light ahead. It had to come from The Villa. That was the only building there. At the same time I heard a car engine behind me. Someone else heading for The Villa, I supposed. I glanced back but, in the haze, could make out only a luminous blur approaching. To keep out of the way and let the driver pass me, I moved well to the side of the narrow road.

In a moment the high beams of the car just about blinded me. I turned my head away and waited for the vehicle to pass. To my surprise, it pulled alongside me. I noticed only that it was a compact and looked vaguely familiar. In the next instant the car lights were turned off and someone shot from the driver's seat and out the door without even bothering to close it. Then I heard steps running around the back of the car and right toward me. I don't know whether it was precognition, but I knew instantly that it was not The Villa this person was interested in, but me.

17

Only Keith's ordeal with the police numbed the shock of Giselle's grisly death. They finally released him, but they still let him know that he was definitely a suspect and was not to leave town. He strongly suspected that but for Don's influence, he would still be locked up.

When he finally had a chance to think, he kept blaming himself. If only he'd gone to her apartment earlier. He was devastated to think that, once again, he'd lost someone he was close to. Now, he felt, he would never find peace until Giselle's murderer was caught and punished.

Apparently her appointment last night was with the same woman he'd seen in the shop on the first day he'd gone there. The minute the police mentioned the name

Olivia Remy, Keith remembered her. Giselle, he recalled, had said something about other psychics consulting her. Giselle must have been doing the same. But why? The answer was patent. Because of him, of course. She'd said something about how she would know what to do, or something of the sort, by the time she returned home. Of course she was talking about the two of them. He'd supposed she intended seeing some psychologist or, at least, some kind of trained therapist. He should have known better. Psychics were *her* therapists.

She had kept the appointment. The police found her datebook and Olivia Remy's name listed in it. When they got in touch with the woman, she confirmed that Giselle had, indeed, consulted her last night. That was all Keith knew, but he could surmise the rest.

Whatever Olivia Remy had told Giselle, she'd obviously made it plain that Keith was not the man for her. Wrong karma or something. Or had she told her something even worse? The way Giselle had rushed back to her apartment, hastily packing a suitcase, and scribbling a quick note, suggested fear, even panic. He could only guess at what had happened. He would never know for sure.

Tonight, when Louise, Don, and he returned from the police station, Bernadette was nowhere in the house. "Where could she have gone?" Louise said, sounding concerned.

Don said, "Maybe she got tired of staying home alone and went over to a friend's house."

"That doesn't seem likely," Louise said.

"She probably went to the store for something," Keith said. "I'm sure she'll be back any minute."

"I suppose you're right," Louise said. "I'll make a quick supper. Don and I should be at work now."

"Don't worry about it," Don said.

When the meal was ready, Keith choked down the food to please her. The last thing he wanted was food. He sat at the kitchen table trying to hide the deep depression he felt.

This was the second time in his life that he'd experienced the death of someone he loved. A fleeting second was all it took to wipe out all that beauty and goodness. Giselle might have been foolish and mistaken in her beliefs, but above all she was a good, kind person. And he was convinced that she did care about him. If only she had let herself love him, she wouldn't have needed to consult some stupid psychic. She would have stayed home, and he would have been with her. No one would have attacked her then.

Louise said, "Keith, I'm so sorry about what happened to that girl. I know that you cared about her. It must have been a terrible shock to find her like that." She reached across the table and pressed his hand comfortingly.

How did she know? Bernadette undoubtedly. He appreciated the fact that she was trying to console him, yet he could say nothing, merely nod. He had lost someone he loved with all his being, and the hurt was too great to talk about. The thought crossed his mind that he and Bernadette had been pretty brutal with Louise, hoping to force her to remove Don from her life. Now, knowing the pain of parting with Giselle, he hated himself. "Louise, I'm sorry about all the things I said when you talked about—about marrying Don. If that's what will make you happy, I want you to know I think it's great."

She patted his hand. "Thanks, Keith."

Don said, "Well, I don't mind telling you that that's a load off my mind. Now if your sister only felt the same, we'd have it made."

"I'll make her understand," Keith said.

"And speaking of Bernadette," Louise said, "I'm really getting worried. I don't know where she could be. Francine was the only friend she visited at home. The only other place she spent time in was the shop, and I don't think she's been there since Francine's death."

Keith was starting to get worried now, too. Her disappearance made no sense. She should have been there, waiting to find out how he'd made out. Not only that, but she knew what time they ate. "I think we should call the police."

Don said, "They tell me that with missing kids, the police won't do anything for twenty-four hours. Why don't we start calling some of her friends?"

Louise said, "She's been very slow about making friends out here. As far as I know Francine was really the only friend she had."

"Then let's start with that store. You said she used to hang around there," Don said.

"What would she go there for?" Louise asked.

With a shrug, Don said, "Who knows? It's just a place to start. Give me the name of the shop, and while I'm calling, you can be thinking of someplace else to try."

They got up and Louise found the number for him in the phone book. While he was dialing, she kept up a running conversation with Keith about all the places Bernadette might have gone, so neither one of them took in Don's conversation.

When Don hung up, to Keith's surprise, he said, "I think we've struck pay dirt. She was there, all right."

"*Was* there?" Keith said.

"About twenty minutes ago, the man who answered the phone said. He said she bought an amulet—isn't that a good-luck charm?"

Keith nodded.

"She said something about taking a bus out to the Peninsula before she left."

"The Peninsula!" Louise exclaimed. "She knows she's not supposed to be out alone after dark. What does she want out there, anyhow?"

Don looked perplexed. "I thought you'd know."

Louise turned to Keith. "Can you think of anyone she'd visit out there?"

The thought flashed through his mind that Giselle, too, had traveled out to the Peninsula to consult some psychic on the last night of her life. Surely Bernadette couldn't be doing anything like that. "Not really. The only person I know of who lives out there is some psychic. I can't see any reason why Bernadette would be consulting her."

"Wait a minute," Don said, and glanced around the room, until he spotted a newspaper lying near the telephone. He snatched it up and opened it for Keith and Louise to see. "It says here that Olivia Remy, a self-proclaimed witch out on the Peninsula, knows who did the murders. This afternoon when I read the article to Bernadette, I thought she seemed impressed with the woman."

"Oh, God," Keith said, "I'll bet that's where she's going. It sounds just like her."

Don said, "You wouldn't happen to know where this woman lives, would you?"

Keith's thoughts turned to the day Giselle had talked about Olivia Remy. Her words came back to him. "She lives in a place called The Villa. It's up in the hills at the end of the road behind the old gatehouse," Keith said. "I have a pretty good idea where the place is. At least, I think I can find it."

"How long will it take us to get out there?"

"In a faster car than my VW, we could probably make it in twenty minutes."

"Good. We'll take my car."

As Keith made for the living room to grab his jacket

from a closet there, he heard Don say to Louise, "Don't worry, we'll find her."

Keith thought of what had happened to Giselle, making the same trip last night. What if they were too late?

18

The moon must have disappeared behind a cloud, because darkness lay everywhere now. Still, I could see
this black shape rushing toward me. For seconds, fear
rooted me to the spot. Then some unconscious survival
instinct took over and I ran, without thought, around
the back of his car and to the driver's side, knowing
only that I had to get away from him. I heard his footsteps pause for a moment on the passenger's side. He
undoubtedly knew exactly where I was and was deciding
what to do about it.

I, too, had to make a decision. And fast. I felt the
amulet for courage. Surely it would protect me, I told
myself. Ahead, I could see a dense patch of fog that
hid even the distant lights of The Villa. If I could just

get that far, he would have a much harder time seeing me. Then it occurred to me that with the light-colored windbreaker I had on, I was all too visible. The burgundy sweater I wore under it and my jeans would give me a better chance to escape in the dark. Quickly, I unzipped the jacket and wriggled out of it. Before I could toss it away, I heard running footsteps behind me. I whirled around, and just as the dark form was almost upon me, I flung the windbreaker over his head, hoping I'd covered his eyes as well.

I didn't wait to find out. Instead, I made a frantic dash ahead, not stopping until I was swallowed in the fog patch. Although I started to tiptoe in what I thought was the right direction for The Villa, my heart pounded so badly I was afraid he would hear it and find me. When, after a short time, there was no sound of footsteps behind me, I began to grow uneasy. Even if he'd taken a few seconds to extricate himself from my jacket, he had to know which direction I'd taken. My running feet would have told him that.

I moved cautiously, silently ahead. Or *was* it ahead? The fog was so thick I could see nothing. The only blessing was that no one could see me either. Yet I had the unsettling feeling that I was losing all sense of direction. On the one hand, I wanted to keep going farther and farther away from him; on the other, I was afraid of making an inadvertent noise and giving my position away. At the same time, I couldn't be sure that

I was heading the right way. Finally, I decided to stay put until I had some reason to feel a little surer of my location.

I shivered and couldn't tell whether it was from fright or from the fact that I had no jacket now. If only the fog would remain on his side and the air would clear on mine. Then, perhaps, I could get to The Villa and yell for help. Surely there could be nothing as bad there as what faced me here.

I waited in silence for what seemed like an hour, my senses keenly alert, listening for a suspicious crackle of a twig or the sound of a pebble displaced. Nothing. I had almost come to believe that my would-be assailant had disappeared or had been only a figment of my imagination. Then I heard the car engine revving. Oh, he was real, all right. I prayed that the fog had forced him to give up and that now he would turn around and leave.

In another moment his high beams cut through my curtain of fog. I shrank toward the shoulder of the road, hoping to stay out of their range. Suddenly the car veered away from its position in the lane and started slowly, deliberately toward me. To my horror, I realized that he not only had seen me but was about to run me down. Desperately I tore ahead now, trying to get away. Behind me the car picked up speed and came at me. I literally dived from the shoulder and into some kind of shrubbery full of brambles. I lay for a moment, stunned, every part of me stinging with hurt.

Then I realized that the car had stopped again. Although the lights were still on and the engine running, I heard the door slam and knew he was coming for me again. The knowledge somehow gave me the strength to free myself from the bush. The fright that overwhelmed me was so great it dulled the pain of my bruised and scratched body as I tore down the road, this time away from The Villa. I could hear running steps hard on my heels.

I didn't get very far. Within seconds I felt a grab at my sweater and arms closing about me. I flailed out to fight him off, but he was too strong for me. After the briefest struggle, I found myself on the ground, something cutting painfully at my back, and him on top of me. I could smell his sweat and sour breath. Although I really couldn't see him, I had the impression that he had no face.

His icy hands closed about my neck and I knew that I was about to die. Like Francine. Like Giselle. The thought flashed through my head that I had brought this on myself by playing with black magic. Another thought hit me. If this was Francine and Giselle's murderer, and I was sure it was, he was certainly not Keith. I could tell even without seeing his face. But that was small comfort to me now.

Expecting his fingers to tighten around my neck, I was surprised to feel him tugging at the chain that held my amulet. The thing resisted him until he gave a powerful jerk that cut into my flesh but wrenched it free. He jumped to his feet and hurled the amulet away from him and into the blackness behind me. Now, I thought bleakly, I have no protection.

Again I was aware of the hurt in my spine. As I used my hands to help me sit up, I felt the wood edge that was poking me. Immediately, I knew what it was. It was the top of one of the risers to the long earthen stairway that Francine and I had ascended so long ago. Before this faceless monster could get to me again, I turned and, feeling my way in the dark, began scrambling up as fast as I could on my hands and knees.

I sensed that I had surprised my attacker, that perhaps he was unaware that the staircase was there and couldn't understand what I was doing now. At any rate, there was a long moment before he followed. By that time, I was on my feet. I remembered that I'd had to take two small steps on the hard-packed earth before I came to the next riser. I could hear him behind me, stumbling, grappling with the unfamiliar spacing of the stairs.

Although I seemed to have the advantage, having made my way up those stairs before, it was not mine for long. The moon suddenly appeared from behind a cloud and cast just enough light to show my assailant the way. Now that he could see where he was going, he moved quickly, closing the distance between us.

In my panic, I found myself scrambling to get to the

top, tripping over risers, and nearly falling again and again. I felt as if I were climbing, climbing and getting nowhere. In seconds he had almost overtaken me. From the step below he made a grab for me and just missed. I turned and, with all the force I could muster, kicked out until my foot met flesh. The impact threw him off-balance and sent him tumbling down the stairs. As he fell, I heard something that sounded like an outraged growl. I wasted no time but tore upward until, at last, I reached the top.

Hoping I'd disabled him, I listened for a moment. To my disappointment, I heard the sound of footsteps pounding up toward me. I turned away, looking for someplace to run to and hide. At that moment I would have welcomed a bunch of Satanists—anyone but the animal who wanted my life. But there was no one, no one at all to help me.

In the hazy moonlight the only thing visible was the Grecian-looking gazebo. Misty fog and dim light combined to cast a ghostly sheen over the Doric pillars. The sight should have convinced me that I was dreaming this nightmare, but I knew better. I dashed for the gazebo and around to the back, where I crouched behind one of the pillars. Whether from the climb or from panic, my breath came in loud gasps that I was afraid would give away my position.

From the sound of his steps, the dry crunch of earth beneath his feet, I could tell that he had reached the top now. Then there was a moment of silence, and I envisioned him surveying the scene, deciding upon his next move. In the small clearing up here there was no place to hide except the gazebo. My only hope was that whichever way he decided to circle it, I would be able to run the opposite way and reach the stairs before him. Then I might have a chance.

To my surprise, instead of making his way behind the gazebo as I'd expected, I heard him mount the steps and go inside. Perhaps he thought I was hiding beneath one of the benches there. As he moved about, obviously looking for me, I decided to risk it now and make a run for it.

Desperately, I tore around the gazebo and headed for the stairs. I'd counted on taking him off guard, but if I had, he soon made up for it. I could hear his running feet close behind me. Before I had even attempted my descent, he was upon me again, knocking me to the ground. He threw himself over me and, in a deep guttural voice, said, "It was you, wasn't it?"

I was so frozen in fear that only a moan issued from my throat. A strange feeling of déjà vu came over me. I had been here before, experienced this horror before. This was the same terror I'd felt here that day with Francine.

"Waaaasn't it?" he shrieked.

I saw the flash of something silver in his hand. A knife! He meant to slash my throat. The realization

206

gave me a new spurt of strength, yet all I could do with it was open my mouth and, at the top of my lungs, scream, scream, scream. Yet I knew there was no one to hear. Even if there had been, a scream here would only be taken for the screech of one of the wild peacocks that roamed the area.

A hand hard over my mouth muffled my cry, but at the same time my instincts responded without thought. My teeth grabbed onto his palm and bit into it so savagely that he snatched away his hand with a yelp. In the next moment he came at me with the knife, and I knew that this was the last moment of my life. I should have known that without the amulet, I had no chance against him. I closed my eyes, accepting my fate.

The stroke that I expected never came. Instead, I was aware of a weight lifted off me, a scuffle, a flashlight shining in my eyes, and someone saying, "Are you all right?"

Seconds passed before I realized the voice belonged to Don. Then I could only nod. As he helped me to my feet, I became aware that someone else was wrestling with the person who had been trying to kill me. Don shone his light that way, and I saw that it was Keith. He had already pinned the attacker's hands behind his back and was ripping what appeared to be a nylon stocking off his head. Don turned the flashlight directly on his face. "Do you know him?" he asked me.

Somehow I was unable to feel any emotion, even surprise, at the sight of the now whimpering creature before me. "Yes," I said, my voice sounding hoarse and strange to my ears. "His name is Mark Keeper."

19

After my rescue on that terrifying night, we all wound up in The Villa, where Don telephoned the police. Mark acted completely docile through it all. He sat in a corner of Olivia Remy's living room, muttering to himself, "I had to do it. I had to do it," while tears streamed down his cheeks. I'm not sure he even realized that he hadn't killed me. In the light Keith recognized him as someone he'd seen near Giselle's apartment building.

If, as she'd claimed, Madame Remy was able to identify the Peninsula killer, there was no evidence of it that night. All she had to say was "Why, he's in my Friday-night class." Mark, it seems, had quit Giselle's class to join hers.

My reaction didn't surface until after Mark was in

custody and we reached home. When Keith told Mother what had happened, she gathered me in her arms. Then I started crying like a baby, and I just couldn't stop trembling. Mother wanted to call a doctor, but when I finally calmed down, I convinced her that I didn't need one, that I was only bruised and scratched. Nevertheless, when Keith mentioned that what I had thought was a knife Mark was carrying was actually a straight razor, I started shaking all over again.

When I pulled myself together, I asked Keith, "How did you ever find me?"

He explained how he had come to team up with Don and head for The Villa. "When we got as far as that creep's car, we had to stop because it was blocking the lane. The lights were on and the engine was running, so I assumed there was something wrong with the driver. I got out to investigate. I also found a jacket on the ground that looked like one of yours."

Don said, "When Keith told me the car door was unlocked and no one was inside, we decided there was something strange going on and we should take a look around. After all, people don't normally abandon their cars that way. I keep a flashlight in my glove compartment. If it hadn't been for that, I would never have spotted the good-luck charm you bought. At least that was what I guessed it was."

"I don't understand," I said.

"When I shone the light around, we discovered the stairway and something glittering a short distance up, on one of the risers." He fished in his suit pocket, pulled out the pendant with the magic squares, and handed it to me. "It was this."

I held it up and stared at it. "I mean, I don't understand how you knew it was mine."

Don told me that when he had called the shop, someone had told him I'd just been there and had bought an amulet pendant.

Keith said, "We decided we'd better have a look at whatever was up those stairs. Before we got to the top, you screamed, and the rest you know."

Only part of it, I thought. In the weeks that followed, though, we found out enough to make at least some suppositions about the murders. Because of Mark's age and mine, the papers never identified us by name, thank goodness. I just didn't want to talk about the experience to anyone but the police and my family. The hearing was private, too.

From what the police learned from Mark, they believe the first girl had hitched a ride out to the Peninsula to sign up for Olivia Remy's tarot class. The ride took her only as far as the gatehouse. Mark, on his way to the class, offered her a lift, which she accepted. Instead of driving to The Villa, though, he took her to the same remote spot, where he killed her.

Although I hated to admit it, I told Keith how I had suggested to Mark that he might be hexed and he seemed to believe he was.

Keith said, "The papers say he claims he's under a

spell and seems obsessed with the idea of killing the witch who did it to him."

"But when we talked about it—his being hexed—that was long after he'd killed the first girl."

"He would have murdered anyhow. You just supplied him with a reason, even if it was belated. In his crazy mixed-up mind, that allowed him to justify what he was doing."

Keith was probably right, I thought. After all, Mark had killed Francine before he'd ever consulted Sammy. Right after he'd left my house that night, he apparently ran into her heading there. Although Keith had dropped her off at her home, she'd never gone in. Instead, she must have decided to accept my invitation to come over and watch television. Of course she knew Mark from the shop, so when he stopped his car and asked if she needed a ride, she asked where he was going. He told her he was headed for the class at The Villa, and she was in just the right mood to join him.

By the time he took on Giselle, he was actively looking for the witch who had hexed him. Unfortunately, Sammy had declared Giselle a witch and had suggested that I had some leanings that way myself.

Naturally, killing Giselle couldn't free Mark from his problems, so he had to look elsewhere for his witch. As he'd told me earlier, he seemed to believe that the person who wished him ill was, as Olivia Remy had told him, someone she knew, someone who consulted

212

her, so everyone he saw at The Villa was suspect. The Friday night that Giselle went out to see her was also the night of the tarot class. One of her assistants taught, but Madame Remy made occasional visits to give inspirational talks to the students as well as to promote future occult classes.

That night she must have finished with Giselle at about the same time the class let out. At any rate, Mark saw Giselle leaving, and with Sammy's words probably still ringing in his ears, he trailed her home and killed her in her apartment. With me, he again made the connection with The Villa. He followed the bus I'd taken and, when I got off where he suspected I would, went after me.

As Keith says, Mark probably would have committed the murders anyhow, but in his deranged mind he could feel more justified when he believed he was avenging some evil deed to himself. I even feel that he might have killed me that night in my home had I not said that Keith would be there any minute. In any case, psychiatrists tested Mark, and he is now in an institution for the criminally insane. I pray he never gets out.

Not long after that horrible night, Keith and I had a long talk about Mother and Don. "You know," he said, "Don is a pretty good guy. If Louise wants to marry him, I don't think we should stand in her way."

Burdened by my feelings of guilt, I broke down then and confessed my crime to Keith, how I'd made the

213

pentagram and how I'd used tarot cards to find out if he was guilty.

"You made a pentagram and tried to call up demons!" he said, sounding as if he couldn't believe it.

"Yes, and every time I tried it, someone was murdered. I just know I'm responsible for all the deaths. I think the only reason I was spared was so that I'd have to live with what I did for the rest of my life."

"Oh, Bunny, you silly kid, how can you believe something that ridiculous?"

"Because I was trying to interfere with other people's destinies—yours and Don's and Mother's. And that was evil. Giselle always said that evil was a great big circle. It just came right back to you."

At the mention of Giselle, I could see a shadow cross his face. Then he shook his head. "You mustn't believe that you had anything to do with these murders. Sure, neither one of us had the right to try to interfere in Louise's life. That wasn't nice, but I wouldn't exactly call it evil."

"Then how come each time I did the incantations someone was murdered?"

"Coincidence. Pure coincidence. And don't forget, the tarot cards were wrong. That should tell you something."

I wanted so much to believe him. Then I remembered how Keith had told me about his feelings of guilt. They seemed a lot like mine. "How about you?" I asked.

214

"Do you still feel you had something to do with Ralph's and your mother's deaths?"

He sighed. "I told you—intellectually, no, emotionally, yes. At least some of the time. Talking to you helped me. I know I have to conquer those feelings, though, just as you have to conquer yours, because they just aren't reasonable. Maybe we can help each other do that."

I said quickly, "Like old times?"

He smiled and nodded. "Like old times. But the first thing you'd better do is stop fooling with all that magical nonsense. It will only hurt you. And not in the way you think, either."

I knew only too well about the getting hurt part, and I had no intention of chancing it again. "You know something, Keith?" I figured if this was a day for confessing, I might as well confess everything.

"What?"

"I know you're right about Willow Orchard. I think I always did. I just didn't want to believe it. That's what makes everything I did even worse."

"Right in what way?"

"I mean, what you said about how it wouldn't be the same anymore, even if we could go back."

"Does that mean you're going to stop fussing about going home?"

I nodded. "It took me a while to figure it out, but I finally did. Home is where you and Mother are."

215

He smiled. "And how about Louise and Don?"

"Don isn't the problem. And if we're going to stay here anyhow, then I don't think it would be so bad if Mother married him."

"Well, I think you should tell her that right away."

"I will," I said.

And I did.

In the four years that have passed since the attack on me, our lives—Mother's, Keith's, and mine—have changed a great deal. Keith is now in med school and will probably, one day, realize his dream of becoming a psychiatrist. I don't think he would have stood a chance without Don's financial help, though. A medical education is so costly. Of course Keith vows he'll pay him back, but Don says he doesn't want the money, that this is what he would have loved doing for a son of his own, had he ever had one.

I don't know how serious it is, but Keith has a girl now. She's a teacher, and like Giselle a divorcee, but without children. She's also four years older than he. I guess he just likes older women.

Mother and Don married soon after my bad experience, as I've come to call it. We live close to the beach now in a big two-story house. Keith gets home as often as he can. We've both come to really respect and like Don.

In all this time I have done as Keith asked and put

216

my dependence on magic behind me. I know now that it has only the power over us that we allow it to have. Yet sometimes I take out the amulet and stare at it and wonder if it was the instrument for saving my life. Then I remind myself that if there are any demons, they are only the ones inside us.